THE  S

A BWWM PREGNANCY ROMANCE
By..

TASHA BLUE

Summary

It was meant to be one hot steamy night but it became much, much more...

Carla has focused all her adult life on her career rather then relationships and it is not something she usually regrets. However, now she is maid of honor at her best friends wedding and she is beginning to wonder when her future husband will ever arrive.

At the reception, while everyone is full of joy, Carla is feeling more lonely then ever. She is surprised to discover that the incredibly dashing best man Daniel is still single himself. And lonely too.

One drink turns into more then a few and the sexual tension between the two of them reaches its peak once they hit the hotel bedroom.

It was supposed to be a one night stand but 2 months later and Carla finds out she is pregnant and now she has some huge decisions to make. Daniel might have been the best man at the wedding but is he the best man for her baby?

Copyright Notice

Contents

Chapter 1

Today more than any other day, Carla was excited to get to the bakery. Her popularity as a specialty cake maker always saw her creating beautiful designs in cream and vanilla, but today she was working on an item with particular significance. Her cousin Diane's wedding was on Sunday and she had asked Carla to make the cake.

Carla stepped into the bakery, smiling and breathed in the delicious scents of marzipan and cocoa, which filled the store. *Carla's Cakes* had a small shop front with glass cases for cupcakes and small pastries to be displayed, but Carla's workroom was the magnificent kitchen through the door behind the counter.

Her young apprentice and store assistant, Lily, was already behind the counter, organizing the cupcake displays and updating the "flavor of the day' chalkboard. She was a young woman just out of her teens with long auburn hair and sweet green eyes. Lily smiled often, which is perhaps why the two got along perfectly.

"Good morning, Lily!" Carla said brightly, as she breezed into the bakery that Friday morning. She was an attractive woman with beautiful dark chocolate-colored skin and long, black hair, which she always wore up to expose the slender slope of her neck. She had bright golden brown eyes and they shone even brighter when she smiled, and that was often. Despite her love of cake and pastry, she had a slender figure with generous curves, and her friends told her more than once that if she would only let go of her fears, the path to true love would definitely run smooth, and then she could have her pick of men.

She flashed a smile at her assistant and waved toward the window.

"The display looks great! Are those the chocolate orange or the cocoa-pralines?"

"A few of both."

"Wonderful! Has it been a busy morning?" Carla asked hopefully.

"The usual rush of school children. Abby came by too to have her regular pre-meeting muffin." Lily told her conversationally.

"Well, she's eating for two now." Carla reminded her.

"She doesn't look like it." Lily said wistfully, patting her own stomach meaningfully.

"She never stops eating and doesn't gain a pound. You know, she came in here last week, ordered a family-size box of éclairs and ate every one while we were talking. Then she bought another box because she was supposed to be taking them to a family party!"

"Well, at least she's keeping us in business," Carla laughed. She cast her eyes around the storefront and, seeing that it was empty, she beckoned Lily to follow her into the kitchen. Lily's eyes lit up in expectation and she eagerly followed Carla into the back of the bakery.

"Are you going to teach me how to do the icing drops?" Lily asked with eager anticipation. Her eyes were wide and hopeful like a child on Christmas morning and she looked at Carla with utter excitement. Carla spoke to her like an affectionate mother to her excitable daughter.

"Not today." she chuckled. "Today I want to show you how to prepare the toppers for a wedding cake. Have you been practicing your sugar craft?"

"I have made so many sugar petals and candied almonds that Pete says it feels like we're living in a gingerbread house." Lily laughed. "I've been practicing molding with clay, but I've been dying to get my hands on some icing."

"Well, here is the design." Carla told her. Her voice took on a careful and conscientious tone as she began to teach. She was a natural tutor; patient and encouraging, and she showed Lily a picture of a cake topper of a bride and groom wearing roller skates.... the bride holding out an arm to help the groom up on his feet.

Lily laughed. "What's the story behind that?"

"Diane and Cliff's first date was at a roller rink," Carla explained. "Cliff was terrible at it and fell over a thousand times, which Diane thought was adorable and the rest is history, I guess."

"That's so sweet." Lily said with a romantic sigh. "I love weddings."

The apprentice leaned back against the counter with dreamy eyes, as she got lost in her romantic thoughts. Carla had to draw her back quickly before her student daydreamed the morning away.

"Where did Pete take you on your first date?" Carla asked her.

"To a dive bar." Lily recalled with a giggle. "He'd never been to that part of town before and thought it looked nice from the outside. We went in and it was full of bikers playing poker and drunks passed out on benches."

"Oh wow." Carla chuckled. "Did you get right out of there?"

"No, we stayed to drink and it was awesome." Lily told her. "After a few shots, we were playing poker ourselves and then Pete walked me home. He was so drunk he could barely stand up straight, but then I was pretty trashed myself. He ended up back at my place because he could not slur out his address to the cab driver. He crashed on the couch and I woke up the next morning to breakfast in bed and flowers. He said he was so sorry to have embarrassed himself, but I just laughed and told him we had fun. He stayed the whole day and we just couldn't stop talking.

We just clicked, you know? He's gotten better at choosing date locations now, but I'll always remember that dive bar as a great laugh. I've said before that I want our wedding reception there, just because it's such a great memory."

"Do you think there's any chance he's going to pop the question soon?" Carla asked with anticipation. "How long have you been together now?"

"Three years." Lily said. "It feels like *for-ever*." She dragged the words out slowly and squeezed at a tube of writing icing restlessly. Lily was like an eternal teenager, always impatient to take the next big step and getting lost in naive daydreams about how perfect everything would be when all her dreams came true in the future, without really paying much attention to the present.

"Do you think he will ask?" Carla wondered, looking at her.

"I don't know." Lily confessed with a dramatic sigh. She paced up and down the kitchen with that youthful agitation she always carried which made Carla feel dizzy from watching her. "I think he wants to get through med school first before we think about anything like that."

"That makes sense." Carla agreed.

"I just get so impatient!" Lily told her. She smoothed some molding chocolate over a polystyrene figure just like Carla was doing, and then picked up a sculpting scalpel to begin to work the chocolate into the shape of a hapless groom while Carla worked on the bride. Her eyes followed the movements of Carla's hands carefully and Carla watched over her attentively, gently offering her advice here and there and then continuing with the conversation.

"He'll get there in the end," Carla assured her in a motherly fashion.

"And what about you?" Lily asked with interest. "It's been a while since we last discussed your love life."

Carla laughed. "My love life?" she repeated. "I'm not looking for anything right now."

"Why not?" Lily insisted. "You're a stunner. You should be fighting them off!"

"I'm not *holding back*." Carla denied. "I'm simply waiting for the right time. I'm waiting for it to find me. I know too many women who just rush into relationships before they have their own lives figured out and they end up stuck under their husbands' thumbs, wishing they had held onto their independence longer."

Lily giggled at her words. "You make it sound like marriage is a prison sentence!" she said. "It's not like you have to choose between your own happiness and your husband's, it's about choosing a husband that makes you happy."

"I know." Carla sighed. Lily's youthful optimism was nice, but Carla was more reserved in her own expectations for love. "I'm sure my time will come, but even if it never does, I'm still doing very well on my own."

Carla liked to think that she believed in love, but in truth, she was a bit disillusioned with the idea of romance. Her parents had divorced when she was very young, which had broken her heart, and then she had a string of bad boyfriends who had cheated on her and disappointed her, which had left her with no real desire to dive back into the dating world and begin it all over again. She saw other people falling in love all the time; she made their wedding cakes, but her own love life was way off track.

"Weddings are a great place to meet people." Lily told her pointedly. "My sister met her husband at a wedding. It's basically speed dating."

Carla laughed. "Is it?"

"Sure it is." Lily insisted. "There's romance in the air; music, dancing, too much alcohol. It's the perfect mix for singles."

"Well, I'll look forward to that." Carla joked. "It's been so long since I went to a wedding. I was a flower girl for my aunt when I was six and then there were a whole bunch a few years ago when everyone started to hit twenty-five. It's like the magic age to settle down."

"How old are you, again?" Lily asked, cocking her head to one side and narrowing her eyes as though she were trying to figure it out. Her scrutiny made

Carla's cheeks get warm and she felt as if she were about a hundred, although there was barely eight years between them.

"Twenty-eight."

Lily made a face before she could stop herself, but Carla couldn't take offense. Lily was barely out of high school, and for her being two years from thirty seemed a lifetime away. Yet, she already had a partner and was thinking about marriage. It made Carla feel like she'd missed the boat, but her apprentice noticed her downcast expression and quickly jumped in to backtrack her words.

"Then again, who wants to get tied down young?" she asked her positively. "You know, you're right. You're an ambitious person. You can rock it on your own."

"You know, when I was younger, I was always looking for a boyfriend and jealous when my friends had guys and I didn't, but once I discovered the baking and started to build my own business, all that feeling like I needed to rush into meeting someone just disappeared." Carla told her. "I've got so many things to focus on now, so much to do for myself; I really don't have the time to give my attention to anyone else right now."

Even as Carla said it, she felt like she was perhaps trying to convince herself a little, too. In truth, she was a very happy person. She built her bakery from scratch after years of teaching herself how to bake and refining her skills so that she could create pure works of art from sugar and butter and had found that she was a natural businesswoman whose friendly nature and constant bright smile drew people to her and her work.

Still, she was a hot-blooded woman just like any other, and there were days when she closed up shop and gone home that she crawled into bed alone and felt like frosting hadn't quite filled a void in her that day.

"I was the other way around." Lily said. "I didn't care about guys at all until I met Pete and then suddenly I had tunnel vision. I'm crazy about him now."

"You guys are so good together." Carla said.

"I should set you up." Lily said mischievously. "Tell me, Carla, what's your type?"

"My type?"

"Yeah, your type; tall, short, stocky, skinny, dark, fair, old, young? Your type?"

"Well, I suppose I like tall men." Carla admitted after a moment's pause. "I like men with nice hair and eyes, but most importantly, I like a man who can make me laugh; make me feel at ease, you know?"

"That is super vague." Lily teased. She began to get into the morning gossip and spoke like a glamor magazine's advice columnist as she carried on chatting with her boss.

"You like a tall man who has 'nice' hair and 'nice' eyes. If that's *it* then it shouldn't be any problem at all for you to find a man."

"He also needs to be able to fit into my life." Carla told her after more consideration. "So many men just want you to drop everything for them. They're not looking for a partner. They're looking for a cheerleader or some arm candy or something. I don't want to be that person. I want a man who sees me and the life I've built for myself and loves it all. I don't want a man who is going to get sulky and jealous because I have to prioritize work or who zones out when I tell him about my new flavors.

I want someone to share my excitement and enthusiasm and not put a downer on it. I also want to be that supportive for someone else. I want to meet a man who captivates me. I want to enjoy his company and smile when he tells me about his work because I can see how much passion is in him. I just want someone who clicks."

"That's all you want?" Lily grinned. "A tall man with nice hair and eyes who likes cake? That's, like, *all* men."

Carla nudged her playfully and leaned over her shoulder to look at her apprentice's work. She gave her some guidance on how to better shape the molding chocolate and they giggled over trying to find a way to make tiny icing roller skates seem authentic. Finally, after a couple of hours of labor, they had produced the perfect comical cake topper. Lily held it up to the light with pride.

"My first cake topper!" she announced. The bride's head was lopsided and her veil askew, which Carla would secretly fix later, but the baker was pleased that all her teaching had paid off and she loved to see Lily get excited about their work.

"You did a great job." Carla praised. "You'll be running this place before I know it."

Lily smiled. Carla had taken her under her wing when Lily had been eighteen and at a loose end in life. She had just lost her mother to illness, was butting heads with her father, and simply didn't know what to do with herself.

Carla had begun speaking to her in an online baking advice forum and soon they'd started chatting on instant messengers. When Carla had found out that Lily lived nearby, she invited her at once to spend a day at the bakery for a trial day and just like that, Lily had fallen into her dream job as an apprentice to the best baker in town. She owed Carla a lot not only as an employer but also as a loyal friend and mentor.

"I'll miss you if you ever move on," Lily told her sincerely. Her lips formed into a heavy pout at the idea. "I know you want to expand and have *Carla's Cakes* all over the place, but it won't be the same here without you."

"Oh, you'll do just fine without me." Carla comforted. "You're great at what you do. I'm always amazed by how quickly you pick up new techniques. Soon you'll be teaching me. If I ever open up a new store you can be sure that I'll be leaving you in charge here."

"You'd trust me with that?" Lily said with disbelief. She tugged at the strings of her apron in a childlike display of hope and looked up at Carla with eyes that were beginning to glaze over as another daydream came to the young apprentice's mind.

"Of course I would, Lily." Carla smiled warmly. "You're my protégée."

Carla had felt an instant connection to Lily when she had begun speaking to her on that online forum. They had begun their friendship talking about icing techniques and cake pops, but once they had started to message outside the forum, Carla had learned that Lily had been through a lot in that last year and she had been so glad that she'd been able to do something to help.

She never regretted it for an instant. Not only was Lily an excellent baker, but she was that encouraging voice at the other end of the phone line after bad news and a shoulder to cry on, even if she was that much younger.

"I want you to do the cake for mine and Pete's wedding, if it ever comes." Lily told her. "I want a cake topper that has us both lying on a poker table with passed out bikers all around and rainbow sponge cake inside the frosting."

"That would get people talking." Carla laughed. She put the cake topper into the walk-in refrigerator and then began to pull out the ingredients for a fresh bunch of cinnamon sultana drops, while Lily popped out to the front of the shop to prepare for the lunchtime rush hour.

Carla thought over their conversation as she whisked together eggs and flour in a bowl. She had been wondering herself lately, if perhaps it was time to seek out a man in her life, but the thought of online dating or cheesy speed dating at a local community center made her cringe.

In a perfect world, she would meet the man of her dreams completely unexpectedly and there would be no drama, no heartbreak, and everything would just come together as though it had always been planned to happen that way. She sighed. The world was not so perfect. If she wanted to meet someone, she had to put herself out there.

The idea was intimidating, at least a little, but as she thought about it, the scent in the air caught her attention. She brought her mind back to what she was doing and focused on her work in the kitchen. After the fresh batch was done, Carla took off her apron and returned to the front of the store to help Lily serve the rush of customers that always arrived for lunch hour. Most were regulars who came in daily from the office block across the street for an afternoon pick-me-up and many had become friends.

"Hello, Linda!" Carla said brightly when she saw one overweight woman in a coat, who always bought two vanilla cupcakes and an éclair. "How are the grandchildren?"

"Very well, thank you, Carla!" Linda beamed back. "How is your mother?"

"She's just fine!"

It was the same with almost every customer that came through those doors. Carla loved to bake, but she also loved to brighten up people's days in other ways and always made that extra effort to have a chat with her customers. Coming to *Carla's Cakes* was like dropping in to see an old friend. When the lunchtime rush was done, Carla let out a long breath and laughed.

"It was busy today!" she commented.

"Well, this place is awesome, Carla." Lily said matter-of-factly. "I know that if I worked in those grim offices across the street that I would be coming here as often as possible to get away. Being in this bakery is like being wrapped up in a warm cinnamon hug."

Carla laughed at the description. "Is it?"

"It is." Lily told her fondly. "Sometimes when I've had a bad day or Pete has driven me up the wall with dirty soccer gear, I lie in bed and imagine that I'm surrounded by cupcakes and all my troubles just melt away."

"Wow." Carla chuckled. "I didn't know this place was having such an effect on you. If you're dreaming in cupcakes, maybe you need some time away!"

"I'll have my time away." Lily assured her. "Just as soon as Pete proposes. Then I can start planning the honeymoon! I want to go to Iceland and see the Northern Lights, or maybe to Canada to see Niagara Falls. Or maybe to the Amazon! Or maybe we should save our money and buy a house... Do you think a honeymoon would be as romantic in a B&B just outside of town?"

"I think you and Pete will be loved up wherever you go." Carla told her fondly. "For what it's worth though, I hear the Northern Lights are beautiful. They have these incredible hotels there, too; made completely of ice."

"That can't be true!"

"I swear on my life it is. I saw it on a documentary."

"A documentary on Iceland?"

"A documentary on unusual hotels."

"Me and Pete in a honeymoon ice-castle, looking up at the stars..." Lily said wistfully. "I just can't wait for him to get down on one knee."

Carla smiled, but felt a little pull in her stomach at Lily's words, which told her that she was lonelier than she would even admit to herself. Carla loved the bakery and everything she was doing in her life, but she wouldn't mind spending a little time in an ice-castle under the skies with a man's arms around her, either.

Chapter 2

Daniel made a face as he looked at himself in the storeroom mirror in a suit that was much too tight and he pulled at the collar to loosen it. The sleeves of the jacket didn't quite reach his wrists, and the pants were clinging to his thick muscular legs.

"I'm not sure this is the right size, Cliff," he said self-consciously. He tugged at the sleeves some more and grimaced at his reflection.

Cliff checked the label and laughed. "No, you're right. That's the pageboy's suit. He's fourteen."

"Well, that's a relief." Daniel said, letting out a long sigh. "I thought I'd put on thirty pounds since giving you my measurements."

The best man stepped back into his changing room cubicle to put on his street clothes, which was actually just another suit, and then he sat on the padded cubes in the waiting area to give his opinion on the groom's suit when he emerged.

Daniel was a very handsome man with piercing blue-gray eyes and dark hair in an expensive cut. He always dressed well and had a careful confidence about him. He had a self-awareness which made every word seem carefully chosen and when his sharp eyes locked on a person, it could be unnerving or remarkably alluring depending on whether he was using his trademark gaze to glare at someone, or invite them to flirt.

Underneath the veneer of the elite businessman, however, Daniel had a good sense of humor, which was often brought to the surface, particularly when he spent time with old college friends such as Cliff.

Cliff came out wearing his chosen grey tailored suit with a black tie and checked himself out in the mirror. He shook out his arms and then his legs and then turned to Daniel with a hopeless shrug. The suit fit him well, but there was an expression of panic on his face which made him look like a child in his Dad's clothes all the same.

"Do you think it looks good?" he asked uncertainly.

"It looks fine, Cliff. You look sharp."

"Does it fit properly, though?" Cliff pressed. "Diane's exact words were 'I am not marrying you if you're wearing the wrong sized suit.' I begged her to come with me so that she can dress me as she wants for the big day, but she said that it's bad luck for the groom to see the bride before the wedding day."

"What?" Daniel laughed. "Isn't that about the wedding dress and only the rule on the night before the wedding? I don't think the superstition extends to the groom's suit-fitting."

"Well, it's too late to change anything now anyway," Cliff said dejectedly. He let out an angry huff at his own reflection and his expression was dissatisfied. "The wedding is on Sunday."

"You look good." Daniel insisted. "She's going to love it. Perfect choice. Amazing."

Cliff cast him a disdainful glance and shrugged off his jacket. He sat on the cube next to Daniel's and let out some of his pre-wedding jitters.

"She wants this day to be perfect." he said. "There are just so many things that can go wrong, though. We've got the florists and the caterers and the musicians and the reception... I'm relying on a hell of a lot of people to get it right."

"They do this for a living, Cliff. They'll get it right." Daniel assured him. "Besides, what's the worst that could happen? If the flowers aren't perfect or the food is late coming out, people will get over it. We're going to be there for you. The ceremony is going to be great. The party's going to be great."

"I didn't think I'd be this nervous." Cliff said anxiously. "I just want this day to be perfect for Diane. She deserves the fairytale wedding and the dream honeymoon that all the girls dream about. I want everything to be just right."

"It's just one day." Daniel told him calmly. "Then you have the rest of your lives together and you're going to have great lives. So why are you worrying? You love Diane, she loves you, and you're going to be happy."

Cliff grinned at him gratefully. "I knew there was a reason I chose you to be my best man," he said. "You're always looking on the bright side. I promise that when you get married, I'll be just as positive as your best man."

"Me married?" Daniel said with somewhat of a scornful chuckle. "That's pretty far off yet, I think."

"What happened to Marcy?"

"God knows." Daniel said coolly. "I went on dates with her and I thought everything was going well, but then she just stopped returning my calls."

"You know, I always got the sense she was a gold digger, anyway." Cliff said pointedly. "She got this gleam in her eyes like a snake whenever you pulled out the credit card."

"No, she was alright." Daniel replied calmly. "Besides, I'm not rich enough for anyone to think it's worth trying to extort anything out of me."

"Are you kidding me?" Cliff laughed. "You earn more than me and my brothers put together. How much did you bring home last year?"

"I'm not telling you that..." Daniel replied, raising his eyebrows slightly as a knowing smile came to his face.

"Because it's some stupidly astronomical figure that will put me to shame," Cliff predicted. He stood up, looked at himself in the mirror again, shook his limbs once more and huffed. He paced back and forth a few times and experimented with doing up all the buttons and then posing this way and that and never seeming to be happy with the cut of the suit.

Daniel shrugged indifferently. "I won some pretty big cases last year."

"You're the superman of corporate law." Cliff said with a tad of envy to his voice. "Geez, I could use those kind of bucks about now with the cost of this wedding."

"I really wanted to help out as a wedding gift," Daniel said earnestly. "You should have let me pay for the band, or the caterers. Or something."

"Never!" Cliff exclaimed. "I just want you there, Dan."

"It's going to be a great day." Daniel insisted confidently. "I just hope you can calm down enough to enjoy it."

"Me too!" Cliff replied. He stood up, did one final spin in front of the mirror, threw his hands up in impatient despair and went into the dressing room to change. Then the two handed their suits to the staff and waited for them to be put into zipper bags.

"You're the only bachelor left from the old crew now." Cliff commented as they waited to receive their suits. "Baz, Will, Tom, Richard, Eddie... All tied down. Then there's you, the most eligible of us all, still just goofing around."

"I work long hours, Cliff," Daniel said to explain himself, looking at his expensive watch with concern even as he said it. "I've always got some deadline or other to meet and the work is stressful and I'm just not good company when my head's in a case."

"You work too hard." That's why you need a nice young lady to come home to. Imagine it: after a long, hard day at the office or the courtroom or wherever you lawyers spend your time, you come home tired, and there's a gorgeous woman waiting for you with her come-hither eyes and a glass of wine. Boom! Troubles gone."

Daniel laughed. "I don't think that's the reality of marriage, Cliff."

"It's not?" Cliff joked in mock surprise. "I better call this thing off, then."

"You can't tell me that everything's perfect with Diane all the time," Daniel said skeptically. "I mean, when you've had a hard day, doesn't it sometimes feel like a chore to come back and have to make time for someone else?"

"It's not like that when you meet the right one." Cliff told him matter-of-factly. "It's like having an extra pair of shoulders to share the load. The right woman doesn't demand anything from you.

I mean, of course you get the stupid little arguments over groceries and toilet seats, but when it comes to the big picture, the right woman will be there for you and it's nice to know that you've got someone to fall back on sometimes. When you've got a busy and hectic life, it's a huge relief when you finally meet someone who can just make it all go away for a while."

"Wow. I didn't know you were such a romantic." Daniel said with a teasing grin. His usual stern business expression broke for a moment to allow it. "It wasn't so long ago that you were in college prowling bars for anyone who'd take you home. You weren't such a romantic then!"

Cliff laughed at the memory and smiled at his friend. "You'll understand when you feel it, Dan," he told him. "You stop even thinking about other women. It's like an off-switch to everything around you but that one person. I used to be the guy going after one not-so-noble thing, but when I met Diane, she kind of transcended that."

"She transcended it?" Daniel scoffed playfully. "You make it sound like a spiritual experience."

The groom shrugged, unashamed. "Meeting the right girl is the moment when everything falls into place. Life comes together. I think that's as close to a spiritual experience as most of us mere mortals ever get."

"I don't know, Cliff." Daniel said doubtfully. "Maybe that fluffy kind of romance just isn't for me. I could never deal with a woman who had a problem with my work and who didn't want to hear about what I do. The right woman for me would have her own ambitions. She would be a confident go-getter who wasn't dependent on me to be her everything.

Unfortunately, most women I meet want to be heard, but never want to listen. I don't enjoy the company of women when it's all one sided. I don't want a woman just for the sake of having someone on my arm. I want someone who fits into my life that I could connect with, but where are you going to find a woman like that?"

"Dating some of them would be a good start." Cliff told him. They were handed their suits at last and headed out into the store's lot to get in the car and head to lunch. "You're incredible with women. I'll never understand it. You swoop in like James Bond, pick up a woman and then it's over in a week."

Daniel shrugged. "It's not getting a woman on a date that's the problem. It's maintaining a connection once you're past all that heat from first attractions. Sometimes I'll meet a woman who seems sexy and sophisticated, but as soon as the seduction is over, it's like a switch flicks and she becomes possessive and demanding and I just pull away."

"You're meeting the wrong kind of women. You always hook up with other lawyers or high-flying consultants or stockbrokers or whatever and you clash. You need someone from a different walk of life so that when you're with her, it's something different than what you're used to."

"I guess I just don't know what I'm looking for." Daniel shrugged. "You tend to just end up around more people like yourself, don't you? I mean there are some really nice female lawyers out there, but it's always a clash of ambitions. Maybe you are right. Dating other legal professionals means you always bring the office home."

"Of course I'm right," Cliff said confidently. "I mean, look at me and Diane. I'm a prosecutor and she's a nurse. We never run out of things to talk about and I'm so attracted to that softness in her. She has such a caring nature, that you don't see when you're tearing out throats in the criminal courts.

I come home and she tells me about people she's met, and the conversations she's had and it makes me smile because she looks so sweet when she's talking about it. She's so gentle. If I came home from a day at court to a woman who was angry because she'd been at court all day too, can you imagine? You'd be squaring off against each other. The house would feel like a battlefield."

"That's what it's like." Daniel agreed. "That's exactly what it's like. Do you remember when I was with Rachelle?"

"I remember."

"Well, I remember one day when we met up after work and my day had been hell because we'd been denied a crucial warrant by the judge and our whole case was falling apart and my client was facing losing his entire company, all because his accountant had been screwing him over.

All I wanted to do was to let off some steam and find some comfort, but Rachelle started going off on one about how her client hadn't gotten some paperwork to her on time and it ended up with us both just raging on without connecting with one another. All my relationships have been like that." Daniel told him.

"Well, there you go." Cliff nodded. "You know what you have to do. Find some nice, down-to-earth woman who has never even so much as watched an episode of *CSI*. A complete breath of fresh air. You need someone who has a calming presence. A masseuse,

Daniel laughed. "You want me to settle down with a masseuse?"

"There have got to be worse things to settle down with. A wife who could massage would be a dream. I asked Diane for a massage once and she poured a load of oil over my back and started digging her elbows into my neck. I had to tell her to stop because it was so awful. Still, at least she can cook."

"I'd appreciate a woman who could cook," Daniel agreed. He unbuttoned his cufflinks in the car and rolled up his sleeves, which was about as relaxed as

Daniel ever appeared to be, and continued to talk with his old friend. "A nice woman who can cook and who smiles a lot so that when you walk in the door, it feels like coming home."

Cliff smiled at him and pulled up outside the restaurant. The two got out of the car, headed inside, and ordered. Cliff looked around at the waitresses who were serving them as his menu was taken and their drinks were brought over.

"How about a waitress?" Cliff suggested. "That one over there looks nice. She is blonde, leggy. Didn't that used to be your type?"

"I never had a type." Daniel said.

"Oh, come on!" Cliff teased. "Let's go back to our college years, shall we: Tammy, blonde; Ira, blonde; Emily, blonde; Georgia, blonde. This is your problem, Dan. You're dating the same woman over and over again. Blonde women of the law, it's a real issue."

"I don't go for blondes on purpose." Dan told him flatly. "They just always seem to find me. I've actually always found dark hair and dark eyes really attractive."

"So we're on the lookout for a woman with dark hair and dark eyes who can cook and is definitely not a lawyer." Cliff reviewed. "I will keep my eye out for you. Hey, maybe you'll meet someone at the wedding."

"Are there going to be many single women there?" Daniel asked with a curiosity that was suddenly piqued.

"On my side, there's only my sister; who is out of bounds for you by the way, and a couple of friends who are your sort of age." Cliff mentally calculated. "Diane's got hundreds of cousins, though. She comes from a big family. I've only met one or two, but I know there were at least twenty on the guest list. I don't know how many are single. Her maid of honor is hot, though. I don't know if she's single."

"'My sort of age'!" Dan repeated with a wry laugh. "Every year there are fewer and fewer singles on the ground who are 'my sort of age'. I feel like turning thirty this year has sealed my eternal status as a bachelor."

"People get married later nowadays." Cliff told him. "Not everybody wants to get hitched young. You've been building a career. Now you can find a woman who appreciates that kind of drive."

"I think it's that kind of drive that discourages women." Dan said. "With all the women I've dated, if we haven't been competing with each other because we're both lawyers, then it's ended because they say I spend too much time working."

"Well, maybe meeting a nice woman would be the perfect excuse to slow down." Cliff said. "You're in high demand now, Dan. You should be able to start to pick and choose cases now. Maybe you could even start your own firm."

"I'd have to go out to the city to do that. It's fair enough working out in the suburbs in one branch of a huge law firm, but starting your own means that you have to be in the center of it all."

"Then go to the city." Cliff shrugged. "If your schedule wasn't so chaotic you could make more time for other things in life, like love. Those things matter too."

"I know they do." Dan agreed. "It's just that I was born to be a lawyer and even when it's tough and demanding and even with the occasional losses, it's that adrenalin rush of a case that gets me going. I couldn't do anything else. I guess I feel like if I want to settle down it would mean giving it all up and getting some quieter nine-to-five desk job which would kill me."

"That's not true." Cliff insisted. "It's just about finding a woman who likes the whole package, including your dedication to your work. She's out there somewhere. I'm sure of it."

"Maybe." Dan shrugged.

"Definitely." Cliff said firmly.

After dinner when Dan had been dropped off outside his elite apartment complex, he entered into his home feeling unsettled by his conversation with the groom.

Cliff was right. Everyone that they had gone to college with was married now and only Dan remained. It wasn't that he didn't want those things himself, because he did, but they were just difficult to come by when he also valued his career so greatly.

Perhaps Cliff was right to say that what he needed was someone completely unlike the other girls he met and perhaps when he found her, he too could experience that moment of transcendence and let life slow down.

Chapter 3

When Diane caught sight of Carla peering around the doorway of the house where the bridal party was spending the night, she let out a squeal of delight and raced across the hall to throw her arms around her cousin in a loving hug and plant a kiss on her cheek.

"Little Carl-la-la!" she cooed. "It's been far too long! How have you been?"

Carla hugged her cousin back tightly and smiled wide. It was good to see her again. They had been as close as sisters growing up, but life had taken them in different directions as they grew older and Carla did not get to see her favorite cousin often enough anymore, although they spoke constantly on the phone and sent each other funny little notes and nonsense gifts in the mail.

"I am fantastic, darling girl!" Carla said warmly. "How are you? Bride to be! You look beautiful as you are. You are going to be a stunning bride."

Diane looped her arm through Carla's and began to lead her through the house and up the stairs to her bedroom. It was her mother's house; Carla's aunt, and Carla had many fond memories of racing around these rooms as a young child playing hide and seek with Diane and playing dress-up in all of her Aunt Tania's clothes.

It made a wave of nostalgia sweep over her when she caught side of Diane's wedding dress hanging at the window and she thought how much time had passed since they had been in the house together as children.

"It has been manic here, but we're getting there." Diane laughed. "I thought I'd be in pieces by now and panicking about all the details, but all I can think about is that tomorrow I'm going to be Cliff's wife."

"I'm so happy for you, Di." Carla said sincerely.

"I wish I could have spent more time with you in the run-up to the day." Diane said regretfully. "I really wanted you to come shopping with me for the wedding dress and to look at all of the bridal magazines together like we used to. Do you remember that?"

"I do," Carla said with a light laugh. "You were going to have a Cinderella wedding and I was going to be Sleeping Beauty."

"Who'd have thought that one day I'd actually be walking down the aisle!" Diane said. Carla looked at her bright smiling face almost brimming over with happiness and felt a stir of envy for the excitement of getting married. Still, she was so happy for Diane who deserved every happiness in the world and so she smiled brightly and hugged her again.

"I just can't wait to see the dress!" she said.

"I can't wait to see the cake!" Diane said eagerly. "How did it come out? Thank you so much for doing it. I know it was probably a pain getting it to the hotel, but I am so proud of you and your wonderful bakery! I just couldn't have had my wedding cake from anywhere else."

"It looks fabulous." Carla assured her. "It's already at the hotel for tomorrow."

"Wonderful!" Diane smiled. "So that means that you're all ready for today! We've got the rehearsal dinner tonight at seven and while it was supposed to be just the bridal party to begin with, there are so many family members that we never get to see that I just decided to have a lot of them join us for dinner, so it's more like a reunion than a bridal party rehearsal dinner.

You're sitting at the high table with me, although the arrangement's a little bit different tonight. We're having the rehearsal dinner in the hotel restaurant, but on Sunday, it will be all laid out in the main hall. It's going to be spectacular. Everything is white and pink, just like we dreamed it would be when we were young. Before that we've got the bridal party lunch."

"I know it's going to be perfect." Carla said warmly.

"Did you have your fitting for the dress last week?" Diane asked her. "Does it look alright?"

"Oh, Diane, it's beautiful!" Carla beamed. The dress was a deep purple, full-length silk gown that made

Carla look she'd stepped off of the cover of a fashion runway magazine. It complemented her skin tone perfectly and clung to her figure in all the right places. Carla was not used to dressing up in formal dresses, but she had felt like a million dollars when she had tried on that dress in the store.

"Purple was always your color." Diane told her with an adoring grin. She tugged at Carla's arm. "Come on! We have so much to do!"

Soon Carla was caught up in a whirlwind of tying ribbons on wedding favors and allowing hairdressers to experiment with different styles on her hair and then, finally, dressed in a simple floral dress and a pair of elegant heels, Carla accompanied the rest of the bridal party to the hotel restaurant for the bridal party lunch.

Arriving at the restaurant and seeing the bridal party made Carla remember why she had turned down the last wedding invitation she had received. There was something incredibly depressing about being single at a wedding.

All the same, Carla told herself to just enjoy the day and let her beautiful smile shine. She looked around at the rest of the bridal party as they began to take their seats and realized that she'd forgotten just how many cousins she had. It took her at least fifteen minutes to take a seat because she kept stopping to catch up with one distant relative or another. It was such a whirlwind that she found herself almost breathless when she sat down at last. She looked around happily as she watched all of her aunts and uncles and cousins kissing and embracing and then turned her attention with curiosity to those people she didn't know. She was so lost in her people-watching that she was startled when someone in the chair beside her,, began to speak.

He was a very attractive man with fair skin and incredible eyes, unlike any Carla had ever seen before. He sat with one leg crossed over the other and an arm casually laid around the back of his chair in a posture, which was relaxed, but still very refined. He wore an expensive suit and the cut of his hair was sophisticated; he looked like a cover of GQ.

He looked to her to be about thirty or so. Everything about him emanated refinement and intellect and Carla felt a little shy to be sitting there in the flowery dress she was wearing with her hair still tousled from the experimenting hands of an indecisive stylist. She felt her cheeks get warm before anything had even been said.

"Bride's side or groom's?" the stranger asked her conversationally. He fixed her with an intense gaze that made it feel to Carla as if she were being held to him by a magnetic pull. Her people-watching stopped. All at once and she was drawn helplessly into deep grey eyes, and captivated by the sophistication of the man speaking to her, so much so, that she stammered over her reply in her shyness.

"B-bride's." she stuttered and then took a nervous sip of her wine to stop her from acting like a fool in front of this handsome man. She cleared her throat slightly, reminded herself that she was a capable and independent person who enjoyed her freedom as a single woman and then sat up straighter, deciding to meet the stranger's gaze with equal intensity and forcing away her shyness. "And you?"

"Groom's."

"A relative?"

"College roommates."

"College?"

"I'm a lawyer, and you?"

"A baker."

The stranger suddenly smiled as though she'd said a magic word and he held out a hand to shake hers.

"I'm Daniel." he said with a wide smile.

She took his and his grip was firm and gentle at the same time.

"Carla." She smiled at him.

He never once let his piercing gaze slide from her face. Even though Carla was trying desperately not to show it, she found her cheeks flushing once more from the instant attraction she felt for this man and something more which was hard to put her finger on; an intrigue maybe.

"What kind of law?"

"Corporate." he told her with an evident pride in his voice.

"Where did you study?"

"Harvard."

"Gosh." she said as her eyebrows rose in admiration.

If Daniel hadn't been speaking with his best friend just a couple of days before about how a different type of woman could change his life, then perhaps Daniel wouldn't have swooped in on the shy and pretty girl in the corner with the warm smile and a dress that wasn't from the latest fashion season.

As it was, he had watched the way that Carla had moved so gracefully from person to person in the restaurant and left every group smiling. He had enjoyed the sight of her slender legs and smooth shoulders in a pretty summer dress and the way her loose hair was slightly tousled. The attraction had been instant, but to find that she was a baker was an extra check in the box and Daniel couldn't remember the last time he had heard anyone say 'gosh'.

He was used to chasing after corporate girls with pencil skirts and stern expressions. This girl in front of him was someone clearly very sweet and demure who had probably never lived a day of the legal high life. This girl was something different.

Suddenly Diane stood up in the center of the restaurant and began clapping her hands loudly to get everybody's attention, and then raising her voice to address them.

"Lunch is about to be served!" she announced. "Please take your seats! Tonight at the rehearsal dinner there will be seating plans - you can find where you are on the board over there - but for now you can sit where you like."

The bride-to-be finished her announcement and then rushed over to Carla to grab her by the hand and usher her into a seat beside her own. Carla was pulled up and away so quickly that she barely had a moment to look back over her shoulder at the handsome man she'd had barely a chance to interact with.

He watched her go with a hungry smile and Carla felt something fluttering deep down in her stomach; a chemistry which was hard to ignore and impossible to forget as the lunch was served.

She kept looking up furtively as she picked at her salmon salad and gazing across the room to where Daniel was sitting with a table of Cliff's college friends. Every time that she looked up she found that he was looking right back at her and every time that she caught his eyes his lips would form an alluring smile which made a heat rise up the back of Carla's neck.

The bride-to-be couldn't help but notice that her maid of honor was distracted and followed her gaze the next time that she looked across the restaurant. Diane smiled knowingly and leaned closer to Carla to whisper in her ear.

"He's charming, isn't he?" she said. "He's Cliff's best man."

"College roommates, he said."

"You've already spoken to him?"

"He introduced himself and we talked for a quick minute." Carla told her. "What's he like?"

"Reserved, sophisticated, and a gentleman." Diane described. "He's also a ladies' man. I can't say I blame him. A guy must have his pick of women when he looks like that."

"Mmm-hmm." Carla found herself murmuring in agreement, before realizing what she was agreeing to and felt her cheeks warm. Diane grinned wickedly; a mischievous bride.

"There are still plenty of hotel rooms left tomorrow," she told her meaningfully. She held her gaze just long enough for Carla to realize what she was suggesting and Carla giggled in shock and playfully nudged her cousin.

"I'm not like that, Diane!" she gasped.

"Daniel has a way with women, that's all I'm saying." Diane warned her. "Cliff tells me how he always has a different woman on his arm. I've seen him with at least three different girls at one point or another myself."

"Thanks for the intel, but I wasn't thinking of doing anything like that." Carla whispered back, blushing. Diane simply laughed knowingly and gave a dismissive shrug.

"Well, I've seen that look in your eye before." she told her. "Tommy Wright. Twelfth grade. Prom finished at midnight and you didn't get home until three."

"There was an after party," Carla said, taking a swift sip of her wine.

"Sure..." Diane teased her with a wink.

Carla made a point after that to not look at the devilishly handsome man anymore, but she could still feel his gaze hot upon her as he continued to watch her from across the room,. After lunch was done and she had returned home to Aunt Tania's house with the other girls in the bridal party, she still found it hard to shake off the feeling of his eyes upon her. It was unnerving to feel so undone by a pair of intense eyes on a very confident man.

The rehearsal dinner was later and Carla was very aware of the fact that apart from her beautiful purple dress, which was being saved for the day of the wedding, she had nothing particularly elegant to wear. Knowing that the handsome, sophisticated man with grey eyes was going to be there, made her want

44

to appear more dressed up than her usual simple dress and apron look.

Unfortunately, all she had was another floral dress for the occasion, albeit a floor-length one this time.

As soon as she returned to the restaurant for the rehearsal dinner that night, she began scanning the area for signs of Daniel, but she didn't have to look for long. She didn't know if it was coincidence, or Diane being mischievous, but her place card at the high table had her sitting right next to a certain Daniel Towler. When the lawyer arrived and noticed with whom he'd be sitting, he looked immediately pleased and pulled out Carla's chair for her before taking his own seat.

"Hello again." he said smoothly, smiling that knowing smile, although what he knew about, Carla couldn't begin to guess. His steady gaze made her skin tingle and she became flustered all over again.

"Hello," she said with a little laugh.

There were bottles of wine laid out intermittently along the table and Daniel reached over to open theirs. He filled up Carla's glass and his own and paid no attention to anyone else at the table as he focused in on her. Carla picked up her glass and quickly took a few sips, hoping to stem her nerves.

Daniel smiled as he watched her become flustered and picked up his own glass with a calm confidence. Carla imagined that he was used to fine dining and drinking good wine. For Carla, life was more of a cup of tea and a cupcake affair.

"So, you're the maid of honor?" he asked her. He spoke the question with a slow and teasing intonation in his voice. It made even the simple question sound like a line, but coming from a man with such a handsome face, it succeeded in its aim of making Carla's stomach flutter once more.

"Diane's cousin." she explained. "And you're the best man."

"It's unfortunate we haven't met before." he told her with a flirtatious gleam in his eye.

"I work hard." Carla said as way of explanation. "I don't see much of Diane anymore."

"You're a baker." Daniel remembered. The words rolled off his tongue as though it gave him pleasure to say them and Carla couldn't imagine why. Daniel struck her more as a man who would prefer a corporate doll on his arm than someone who spent her time in less lucrative pursuits.

"And you're a lawyer," she stated, in order to break away from the intensity of his interest in her and to turn the attention onto him. "What kind of law do you practice?" she asked, turning the tables to take the pressure from herself.

Talking about himself seemed to break the spell a little. The lawyer sat back on his chair as he had done earlier that day, with one leg over the other and one arm over the back of the chair as though he owned the place. He felt at ease, making himself comfortable, while Carla sat up straight on the edge of her chair, trying desperately to seem sophisticated and well-mannered in his presence.

"I work in corporate law." he told her.

"Gosh. That sounds challenging," she said.

"Actually, it's thrilling." Daniel told her. The lawyer sat forwards as he began to tell her about his work and his eyes lit up as he did. He told her all about his high-profile cases, his millionaire clients, and the businesses he had seen be made and broken in the courtrooms he worked in, and Carla was utterly captivated by the way he spoke.

There was confidence in every word that crossed his lips and as he told her of his work.

Carla was in awe of his intelligence, prowess and knowledge of the law. She felt like a little bird sitting next to a tiger, but the power in him was addictive.

She was drawn to it more than she had ever been drawn to anything in her life. She barely understood a word he said about the legal complexities of his cases, but she could have listened to him speak forever.

"Enough about me." He sat back against his chair and looked at her with an interested smile. "I want to hear about you."

Carla laughed shyly. "What do you want to know?"

"How did you discover baking? Where do you work? Tell me everything." He gave her a little laugh and it eased her tension some.

"Well, after high school I was working as an assistant in a food store." Carla told him. "I was bored out of my mind. There were these free magazines that were delivered to the store each week and they had recipes and articles about cooking and baking in them. I used to read them to pass the time and then I started to try out a few of the recipes and I just found I was a natural at baking.

I started to find myself baking in all my free time until eventually it was all I wanted to do. I quit my job and started to bake full time. At first I was just selling out of my home to friends and family, and going to festivals and things like that, but then eventually I decided to just go for it and put everything I had into opening the bakery.

It nearly bankrupted me at first, but I got through the first year and then it was like something clicked and it worked like a charm. I've never looked back." She smiled in a little self-satisfaction. She was proud of what she had accomplished by working with such dedication, and she was not afraid to show it.

"I admire a woman who works hard for what she wants." Daniel told her. He smiled at her in appreciation, but there was something devilish in his eyes making it seem like there was more to his words than he spoke aloud. There was a sexual tension building between them that made everything feel like it had a double meaning.

It was unlike Carla to find herself flirting with a man; she had abstained for too long, but now she felt like, perhaps it was time to take what she wanted and her thoughts turned to Diane's suggestion of a hotel room. She quickly pushed the thought away and cleared her throat as her heart beat a little faster and she drank more wine.

The rest of the dinner passed with plenty of good food, good wine, speeches, and a simmering heat between Carla and Daniel, and Carla tried to hold back from it. Daniel, on the other hand, was determined to follow Cliff's advice and pursue a woman of a different lifestyle.

Carla was sweet and open and ambitious for the simple pleasures in life, rather than wanting to take over the world in a blaze of glory. She had dark hair, dark brown eyes with light flecks of gold, she could cook and she was definitely not a lawyer.

Daniel found himself wildly attracted to her and he didn't know if it was because in the back of his mind, Cliff had challenged him to step outside his usual conquests.

Or was it because Carla was delicate and sensual at the same time in a way that Daniel had never seen before. Either way, his sights were set on her, and his body was reacting to her. Desire for her had begun to well l up in him, and it was strong.

Sleep that night didn't come easily to Carla because her thoughts were too much on Daniel. She felt like she had been singled from the crowd for impure purposes and where that kind of presumption would usually make her frown and save herself for someone with nobler intents. However, when it came to Daniel, she felt the presumption was fairly placed.

She was intoxicated with him and she ached for the wedding the next day, not for the ceremony so much, or to see people enjoying her cake, or even for the chance to catch the bouquet when it was tossed. It was for the minute possibility that Daniel would ask her to dance. She wanted to know what it felt like to press her body close to his.

Carla laughed at herself as she lay on the bed in the bedroom she had always stayed in when visiting as a child and put a hand to her face to cool her own flushing cheeks. It was so unlike Carla to let her attractions get the better of her, but then again, her attractions had never been quite this strong.

The next day, Carla tried to pull her thoughts away from Daniel so that she could enjoy the company of her female relatives and she joined in with the electric atmosphere that always accompanies a group of women preparing for a wedding.

Diane looked gorgeous in her dress with her hair arranged like a plaited crown atop her head, held in place with a stunning tiara, and Carla gave an appreciative glance to her own reflection in the mirror, thinking that she didn't look so bad herself in the dress that made her look so sexy.

She wore her own hair up with a few loose tendrils hanging down and took extra care with her make-up to make her eyes seem large and alluring, as she felt that they were her best feature.

With her heels, her makeup, and her sophisticated purple gown, she felt that perhaps the elite Mr. Towler was not so far out of her league after all.

They were on separate sides of the church during the ceremony and she tried not to look across at him as her cousin exchanged her vows. When the ceremony was over and the bridal party began to gather for the photos, the groomsmen were asked to stand in a row behind and the bridesmaids were placed in a row in front of them.

Daniel made it seem as though his place behind her was by chance, even though Carla had spotted him stepping away from a woman who had been much closer to be her partner in the photo and then he stood closer to her than needed as the camera flashed, but she didn't step away.

Then it was time for the real dinner and Carla and Daniel were sitting together once more. He poured wine for her as he had done the day before, and this time Carla drank it down for the heady feeling it brought, and just so that she could let her inhibitions slide away for something she knew she wanted.

All through the dinner, he charmed her and as she drank more, Carla found herself responding to his advances with equal flirtation, until finally, they were on the dance floor together. When the slow dances came on at the end of the night, Daniel put his arm around Carla's waist, pulling her towards him closely, and she put her arms around his neck and let her fingers run through the hair at the base of his neck in a flirtatious manner.

That was so unlike her, but it came naturally through the wine and her attraction to him. He seemed to enjoy her touch and leaned in to whisper in her ear as they danced.

"You look absolutely stunning tonight, Carla," he told her in a low, alluring voice. "It may sound selfish, but I almost wish you had done all of this," he looked her up and down from head to toe,... for me."

She felt heady and strong, free and sexy as hell, as his eyes traveled over her. His hands moved from her waist down lower on her hips and he held her snugly to him. The chemistry between them began to burn warmly as he rubbed his fingertips against her lower back and brushed his lips over the line of her jaw.

It made her close her eyes as her body tensed with need and heat and she made up her mind then that she wasn't going to let this night and the chance for something incredible with the beautiful man in her arms slip away from her.

She looked up at him through her thick dark eyelashes and in a soft voice she said, "I didn't put it all together for you, but I wouldn't mind taking it all apart for you." Her heart beat heavily against her chest and in her mind, she was shocked at herself for saying something so bold, while simultaneously feeling a huge rush of satisfaction at speaking so honestly.

Surprise and hunger flashed in his eyes and he looked from her steady gaze to her full lips, thinking how much he wanted to taste them, and then he met her eyes again. "Is that an offer?" he asked in a quiet and serious tone.

Carla nodded and she felt his hands tighten on her body, sending her insides spiraling in chaos.

"I'm ready anytime you are. I don't like to keep a lady waiting." The corners of his mouth turned up in a smile and his eyes twinkled at her. "I'm sure that I could secure accommodations upstairs if that would suit you," he said looking at her with intense heat in his grey eyes.

His look made her stomach tighten, and her heart beat faster, and she smiled back at him. "Let's call it a night," she intoned with a velvety voice.

He stopped dancing but didn't let her go right away. "I'll meet you at the elevators," he said quietly.

Daniel let her go as the music stopped and they walked away from each other as if nothing was going on, but everything was going wild within Carla. She couldn't believe she was going to do what she was about to do, and she was so glad that she was doing it.

She picked up her clutch and kissed some of her cousins goodbye, and then left the reception and walked to the elevators. His back was facing her as she approached him, but at the sound of her heels on the floor, he turned in place to look at her, and as he watched her walking toward him, he was simply astounded by her grace and beauty.

The most attractive part of it was that it came naturally to her. She wasn't trying to walk with a sexy strut, or do anything out of her nature; she was just being herself, and it made her shine like a diamond. It struck him as ironic that so many of the women he went for put on airs and did their best to act like sex kittens with him, but this one, this woman, she blew all of the other women away with no effort at all, and it struck him to his core.

She reached the elevator and he entered it behind her. The doors closed, and the moment they were alone, he faced her, leaning intimately close to her, as her back was pressed up against the wall of the elevator. He lifted his hands to cup her cheeks, and tilted her mouth up to his.

Daniel didn't kiss her right away; instead, he brushed his lips softly against hers, back and forth for a moment, feeling them before touching the tip of his tongue to them and tasting her.

Carla felt like he was setting her on fire and she gasped as their tongues met and his mouth closed over hers, kissing her slowly and sensually while his hands rested low on the front of her hips, holding them and squeezing her firmly. The pressure of his grasp sent shock waves through her and she felt heat flood every part of her as her desire flamed for him.

He lifted his mouth from hers and looked at her with a raw hunger that caught her off guard. His swollen lips were parted and his breathing was heavy, as his eyes penetrated hers.

"I've been wanting to kiss you since I saw you. That was so much better than I imagined it would be,' he whispered to her in a husky voice, leaning back slowly and standing away from her with his grey eyes locked on her.

Carla's chest rose and fell rapidly as she tried to get her breath back, staring at him and almost panting with the heat between them.

They shared their intense gaze as the elevator came to a stop and Carla's mind began to go wild with wonder, excitement, and anticipation about what was about to happen. Her heart thudded heavily against her chest as the elevator slowed and the doors opened, and Daniel finally took his eyes from hers, taking her hand in his and leading her to the room he'd gotten for them.

In no time, the door of the room was closing behind them, and as it did, Daniel wasted no time at all. He pulled Carla into his arms and kissed her again, harder and hungrier this time, and she responded in kind, sucking and biting at his mouth as her desires burned in her with a white hot flame.

They made their way slowly to the bed as he pulled his clothes off a piece at a time, and when she reached for her zipper, he closed his hands around hers and whispered breathlessly, "Oh no... I want the privilege of peeling that dress off of your gorgeous body." He moved his mouth from hers, trailing kisses to her ear and her neck, stealing her breath as he blazed fires of need in her skin.

 She was euphoric, standing so near him, feeling his ravenous hunger for her and her own ache for him, which was almost too much for her to control. Yanking off the last of his clothes, he stood before her, nude and aroused. She let her eyes fall from his, wandering over his body and drawing in her breath as she took in his strong lines and hardened muscles. It was obvious that Daniel worked hard to maintain a chiseled physique.

He watched her looking at him, proud of his body, and anxious for her to be intimate with it. He saw her mouth open in awe at him, he saw her catch her breath, and as her warm brown eyes rose back up to meet his gaze, he felt like his skin might have caught on fire.

It was the first time a woman had looked at him that way. They all gawked and stared, they all lusted after him; he knew he was beautiful, but no woman had ever looked so surprised in such a sweet and almost innocent way; and way that made him burn for her, wanting to share with her what she had found amazing. It was an unusual sensation for him, and he wanted more of it.

He lifted his hands and ran them from her bare shoulders down to the sides of her breasts, tracing them over the material that hugged her like a second skin. A soft sigh sounded from her lips as he held her gaze.

"I've never felt so turned on just by a woman looking at me." A smile spread over his lips. He slid his hands around behind her and slowly unzipped her dress as he left teasing little kisses along her neck and the top swell of her covered breasts.

The zipper down, he leaned back and slid her dress off her, revealing her body to him. All that she had on underneath were little lavender lace panties and his smile faded from his face as his eyes took her in.

His expression changed to one of voracious need. He let his hands move over her, from her shoulders to her fully rounded breasts and hardened nipples, down over her ribs and belly to the curve of her hips.

Carla closed her eyes as he sculpted her with his hands, drinking in the feel of his touch and the profound measure of his desire for her. She raised her hands to touch him, laying them flat on his chest and sliding them down his solid form to his thick erection, and as she closed her hands around it, he groaned in his chest and pulled her to him, holding her tightly as he lowered her to the bed and hovered above her.

Daniel kissed her mouth passionately, pushing and pulling at her lips as his hands began to move over her skin, squeezing and massaging her. Everything in her yearned for him and it only grew more intense as his mouth moved to her breasts, sucking and biting at them, and then over her belly, to the hem of her panties.

He teased her then, pulling them ever so lightly from her skin, just at the top, and kissing where the material had been. She sighed sweetly and he pulled the material further away from her, sliding her last article of clothing off her body. He replaced the lace with kisses and nibbles, making her gasp as he pulled the piece from her, leaving her nude before him.

He lost no time in sliding his hands down the length of her thighs to her knees, pushing them apart, and dipping his head to meet her. He kissed her softly at first, and then with growing urgency as the flames of passion became a bonfire between them. His tongue maneuvered all over the outside of her, and into her soft folds of her, making her arch her back and twist her fingers in his hair.

His hunger for her was insatiable, and the heat and strength of his tongue moving against her made her cry out and come, gasping for air and closing her eyes in the release.

At the sound of her orgasm, Daniel could hold himself back from her no longer, and he moved above her and thrust himself into her depths, filling her and holding her tightly against him.

Carla clutched at his shoulders to anchor herself in their storm of passion, as they moved together, their bodies stiff and taut as they wrestled and moved against each other, both of them lost in the tidal waves of pleasure that overtook them. At long last he could not keep his passion at bay and he cried out as he flooded her depths with his orgasm, clinging to her and holding her against him, as they trembled and shuddered with the final throes of their wild need.

Finally sated, they fell back weakly into the bed and sighed, each one catching their breath as their bodies slowed and peace enveloped them.

Chapter 4

Carla nestled against Daniel's strong chest and felt completely satisfied. They slept long and deeply, and in the early hours of the morning, she opened her eyes, feeling him beneath her and wondering in amazement at what they had shared.

As the light began to filter through the blinds of the hotel window, she began to feel a little disappointed that it was over. This was the first time in years that she had given in to pleasure without thinking about how it might leave her wanting.

She stretched out her body and then turned to lay against Daniel's chest again. Her movement caused him to stir awake and when he spotted her, his lips formed an equally satisfied smile.

"Good morning." he said.

"Hi." Carla smiled.

Daniel looked over at the window and saw that it was already day. He sighed with disappointment, but then sat up in bed and rubbed his eyes.

"That wasn't like me at all," Carla told him shyly. "It's going to sound trite, but I really don't usually do this kind of thing."

The same couldn't be said for the lawyer, but he smiled understandingly all the same.

"There's nothing wrong with enjoying yourself. You did enjoy yourself, didn't you?" His voice was slow and teasing again.

"You know I did," Carla replied, with a self-conscious giggle. "But it was just for fun. I am not really looking for anything serious right now."

Carla was sure that Daniel hadn't expected their one-night stand to turn into a relationship, but she still felt like she needed to express, that for her, this had been a one time affair. She had the feeling that Daniel had had many one-night stands and that he wasn't looking to get tied down to any woman, no matter how electric his night with her had been.

But she still wanted to make it clear by saying it out loud. Carla had enjoyed the night thoroughly, but a playboy didn't fit into her long term plans and she didn't want to walk into another heartbreak by falling for a man who was nothing like her.

"It was fun," Daniel agreed, "but not all things have to turn into something serious. Don't look so worried about it. You had a good time and so did I; aren't we lucky for that."

He leaned over and kissed her softly and she kissed him back. Daniel looked at her with a grin and said, "thank you for a really incredible night."

The baker smiled and was satisfied with that. Sure, it would be nice if mind-blowing nights like the one before came more often. But she knew that sex like that always came with strings attached, so she was happy to just let this be a wonderful and deeply sensual memory.

They went their separate ways after that, and there was no awkwardness between them. Daniel even kissed her once more before she left the hotel room ahead of him. When she was gone, Daniel smiled to himself. Cliff had been right. His encounter with Carla had been unforgettable, but the timing was not right to try to build a relationship with someone new and unfamiliar.

Carla arrived back at the bakery late on Monday afternoon, which made Lily ask a thousand questions about the wedding.

"You hooked up, didn't you?" she gasped. Her voice was shocked. Her boss had never so much as been on a quiet date with a dull man, let alone had a steamy one-night stand with a stranger.

The baker grinned and giggled, giving herself away, and Lily's eyes grew wide.

"Spill it!" Lily demanded impatiently. She began to tense in anticipation for the news and grew more and more restless as Carla took her time in telling her what had happened.

"Oh, come on!" Lily urged her. "Start with the basics. Who was he?"

"The best man." Carla confessed.

"Was he tall with nice hair and eyes?" Lily grinned and folded her hands together.

"Very tall, stylish hair, and about the most amazing eyes I've ever seen."

"So, what happened?" Lily could not contain herself.

Carla shrugged self-consciously and giggled again, shy to be telling this story to her apprentice who was hanging onto her every word.

"He was charming and sophisticated and I suppose I just let go of my inhibitions a little." Carla told her, and then corrected herself. "Maybe a lot."

"He must have been some player to get you interested!" Lily exclaimed. "I've seen a hundred guys hit on you and you always turn them away. You always talk about men being trouble. What was different about him?"

"Oh, I don't know." Carla gave a distant sigh." I suppose it was his confidence. He spoke to me like he already knew what was going to happen that night and I thought he was so... *daring* that I couldn't help but get drawn in."

"Daring?" Lily repeated excitedly. "So what happens now? Are you going to see him again?"

"No." Carla said firmly, her eyes serious. "You're right. I think men are trouble and especially this one. He's a player and some big shot lawyer. It was nice to live in the fantasy for a night, but he would never go for a simple woman like me, and I wouldn't want to invite that kind of trouble into my life. I've got my life all worked out and he would only shake things up. I told him it was a one-time thing."

"What's so wrong with shaking things up?" Lily urged her. "You're great, Carla, but you forget you're young sometimes. You should be taking risks and stuff now, before you *are* old and it's too late."

Carla laughed. "I wish I had your attitude, Lily," she said. "It's just that I like my life the way it is. I just want to keep on building what I have and open a new bakery. I'm the only one that's going to make that happen."

Lily sighed despondently. "I got excited that you were going to tell me you'd met someone to get you out of your shell a little more."

"I was pretty out of my shell last night," Carla said meaningfully, making Lily forget that the gossip wasn't as juicy as she had hoped, and she laughed. The two carried on with their day and Carla tried to forget about the feel of Daniel's hands on her body and his breath on her neck, although the memories came back to her in sweet waves of sensation that made her smile without noticing, although Lily kept casting her knowing glances.

Uptown, Daniel didn't talk about Carla again until Cliff had returned from his honeymoon and they met up for a drink at an expensive bar near Daniel's apartment. Cliff wasted no time in getting to the matter at hand.

"Diane told me that you stayed the night at the hotel with her maid of honor. Well?" Cliff leaned forward and prompted Daniel to speak with an impatient hand gesture and then huffed when Daniel made him wait.

His friend sat back on his bar stool with a cool and self-satisfied smile and Cliff rolled his eyes.

"Typical." he said. "Why is it so easy for you? Why would a nice girl like Carla want to take a risk with a guy like you? Diane said she's just not the type."

Daniel laughed. "She had no complaints."

"God, you're so slick." Cliff told him with a shake of his head. "You're just too smooth, you know that?"

"I know that."

"Of course you know that," Cliff sighed. "So, what now? Are you going to see her again?"

"No." Daniel said. "She wasn't interested and I had second thoughts about this different girl idea. She's a baker, Cliff. Can you imagine me with a girl like that? If I was desperate to settle down and marry someone tomorrow, maybe I'd had taken her on a date and see how things could be with her, but right now it just doesn't seem like the right thing to pursue."

"Oh, don't pretend that you pulled away because you just had too many options." Cliff scolded him. "You chickened out."

"You think?" Daniel asked with a single raised eyebrow.

"I know," Cliff insisted, looking at him seriously. "You met a regular, sweet, nice young woman who isn't going to be impressed with all this... "

He threw his hands in Daniel's direction as he searched for the word, "*flash*.., and you got scared that you'd met your match."

"Not at all." Daniel said with a shake of his head.

"'Not at all'." Cliff parroted. "You know I'm right."

Daniel hadn't considered it, but maybe Cliff was right. Dan knew that his perfected appearance, expensive suits and impressive career had always helped him to draw the admiration of women from his field, but perhaps he was a bit uncertain about whether a woman who wasn't part of the high rolling world he lived in, would still like him when she wasn't dazzled by his reputation and lifestyle.

"I think it was just the wrong time for her," Daniel said, pushing his self-doubts away. "She's running her own business."

"And you're busy too. I've heard it all before. There's got to come a day when that's not an excuse anymore.

I think you should call this woman and take her out on a real date. Spend time with a nice down-to-earth girl for a change."

"No. It's too late for that." Dan told him.

"What do you mean?"

"I'm dating Brooke from Holland & West."

Cliff looked at him in surprise and lowered his brow curiously.

"The lawyer from the other company in the merger?"

"That's the one," Daniel said with a tilt of his head.

"Let me guess. She's blonde?" Cliff gave a half smile.

Daniel sighed under the inquisition and shrugged unapologetically. "It makes more sense to date someone who does what I do." Dan told him.

"No. It doesn't." Cliff argued. "It's convenient, but it stops being convenient the second you realize that someone as stubborn as you gives you a headache." He pointed his finger in the air to punctuate his statement.

"That's enough about me," Daniel said quickly, to change the course of the conversation. "How as the honeymoon?"

Cliff eased back and smiled then, letting go of some of the frustrations towards his friend, who he thought always made bad choices when it came to women.

"It was perfect," he said. "Just Diane and I with nothing to worry about." He took a swig from an expensive artisan beer and then sighed despondently. "I suppose it won't last, though." he said. "Diane's already started to talk about having kids."

Daniel chuckled at his friend's predicament and took a swig of his own brew.

"That's marriage," he said. He looked at his watch and drank down the last of his beer. "I'm sorry, Cliff, I have to go. I'm meeting Brooke across town in twenty minutes."

Cliff waved his hand in a gesture of goodbye and stayed to finish his drink. Daniel stepped outside and flagged down a cab to meet Brooke at a restaurant. She was waiting for him on the sidewalk outside with a beautiful dress and a stormy expression.

She was a beautiful woman. She had long blonde hair, which hung in a smooth layer, spilling over her shoulders and framing a face which was the classic picture of beauty. She had light eyes with long lashes and she wore red lipstick, which highlighted her impatient pout. Daniel raced across the road and kissed her formally on the cheek.

"Sorry I'm late." he apologized.

"Where have you been?" Brooke snapped. "It's freezing out here. I've been waiting forever."

"It's mild, darling, and I'm ten minutes late," he replied calmly. In all his years of dating high-maintenance and entitled women, he had developed a skilled patience for them. He expected snappiness and ingratitude from them, but reasoned that a little selfishness from a woman was a small price to pay for the pleasure of having a beautiful woman and a partner who fit comfortably into his life without him needing to make any adjustments. "Let's go inside."

Brooke stormed ahead and didn't thank Daniel when he held open the door for her. She sat down at the table and only stopped her sulking when he ordered an expensive bottle of wine, which made her attitude change.

"Oh, I'm sorry, darling, for snapping," she drawled, reaching across the table to squeeze his hands patronizingly. "I'm just so hungry after the case review this afternoon and absolutely nothing has gone according to plan today. My associate did nothing she was supposed to do. The girl is useless! Honestly, these girls get a degree from a reputable college and thinks it makes them invincible.

Well, I told her straight out, I said, 'Olivia, this apathy will not do. You better get your act together or I will kick you right to the curb and you know that associate positions are hard to come by. Good luck finding another lawyer of my status to take you under her wing!'

Well, obviously, she started crying and I just had no sympathy for her. I mean, does she think the law is a stroll in the park? She is going to be fighting bigger, meaner people than me in court so she better get used to people telling her the truth."

"Didn't you tell me that your associate was just off work because her brother died?" Daniel recalled with a frown.

"So?" she looked at him quizzically.

"Well, maybe that is why she's been struggling," he offered generously.

"Oh no, darling," she said, waving her hand. "She's struggling because she's not as smart as she thinks she is." Brooke added spitefully, "Besides, do you think anyone else will go easy on her just because of a bereavement? Would she drop a multi-million dollar case because she's having a hard time? It doesn't work like that at all and, as her mentor, I have to make sure she understands the way it goes. I'm doing her an enormous favor."

Daniel sighed and didn't argue with her. Brooke was a hard lady with sharp edges, but Daniel liked the fact that she was independent and didn't complain when he worked long hours. She worked near his offices and so it was easy to see her after business hours or during lunch and she it didn't hurt at all that she was stunning.

Unfortunately, Daniel's criteria for meeting women were rarely more specific than these, which was why he so often dated women who made him unhappy. Even as he listened to Brooke drone on about how all her colleagues were incompetent, his thoughts turned to Carla who had made everyone smile as she passed them e that day at the wedding. She was in such sharp contrast to these power-hungry corporate women he dated who had superficial beauty, but deep character flaws.

He didn't get much chance to speak himself on that date and afterwards, Brooke came back to his apartment for a mechanical encounter in the bedroom and a quick goodbye. Afterwards, Daniel felt unsatisfied and bored and could only think of how different things had been with Carla that night.

It was two months after the wedding and Carla hadn't gotten Daniel out of her mind either, but there were about to be far greater things on her mind. Missing one period could be explained away as stress or illness, but missing two was cause for concern.

Carla hadn't wanted to test herself for pregnancy because the thought of being left with a child after a one-night stand made her head spin in panic. However, after the test had been done more than once and a tearful doctor's visit had confirmed the suspicion, Carla could no longer escape from the fact that she was pregnant. Lily was the first to know.

"Oh God, Carla!" she exclaimed so loudly that Carla had to shush her before she drew attention. "What are you going to do?"

"I don't know!" Carla had whispered desperately, constantly looking over her shoulder as though expecting to see her customers huddled around the counter, trying to hear the juicy details. "What can I do?"

"Are you going to keep it?" Lily asked with wide eyes.

"Yes." Carla sighed. "Definitely."

"I dunno, Carla. I mean, well, you said it; what can you do? I can come with you to buy a crib or something. Would that help?"

Lily tried to be supportive and comforting.

Carla didn't have a great relationship with a loving partner to ease the worry and work brought on by a surprise baby, and her small apartment above the bakery was no place to raise a child. Where was the baby going to go while she was working? Carla put a hand to her head as a hot flash came over her and Lily ushered her into the walk-in refrigerator to cool down.

There, among the chilled towers of wedding cakes and the dozens of brides and grooms staring at her from the cake-topper shelf, the night of the wedding came rushing back to her.

"I'll have to track him down." she stated. "I'll have to tell him."

"Good, good!" Lily encouraged. "You should go now. Do you want me to come?"

Carla smiled weakly at her concern, but shook her head.

"No, honey. You stay here and watch the store," she told her. "Do you think you'd be able to make a few fresh batches? I wrote this week's recipes on the whiteboard above the equipment bank."

"I can handle it." Lily promised her. Suddenly, the young girl who had such a taste for drama and gossip became serious and laid a hand on Carla's arm to comfort her. "It's going to be OK. I'm going to be here with you through all of this."

The baker smiled again and sighed as she stood up to leave. She knew that Daniel worked at Banks & Porter, which was uptown. She hailed a cab on the main street and headed there. Perhaps it wasn't the greatest idea to confront him with the news in his office, but Carla didn't have his number and she certainly didn't want to call Diane to ask for it. She arrived at the office late in the afternoon and stepped into the foyer of the elite law firm.

The building was all glass and chrome. It looked like something from the future in its design and everybody was wearing a pristine suit and rushing in all directions with purposeful strides and armfuls of paper. Carla felt so out of place with her simple dress and shy steps. She went to the reception and asked for Daniel Towler.

"Do you have an appointment?" the receptionist asked curtly.

"Well, no, but he knows me." Carla told her.

"I'm sorry, ma'am, but I can't let you in without an appointment."

Carla was in the middle of protesting when she felt an arm on her shoulder and turned to see Daniel standing behind her. She lost her breath all over again, seeing him as handsome as he'd been that night, and almost at once she was lost in his eyes.

"It's alright, Natalie." he told the receptionist. "She's with me."

He nodded towards the elevators to suggest that Carla should follow him there. Once they were in the elevator, alone together, Daniel looked her over with cool eyes that revealed a slight surprise, although Carla wasn't sure if he was pleased to see her. She thought for a moment of the last time they were in an elevator together and the heat of the memory made her heart beat faster.

"Not that I'm not glad to see you, but it's a surprise to find you here," he told her with a kind smile.

The elevator arrived at the twelfth floor and the doors opened. Daniel gestured for her to go ahead and he followed her to the twelfth floor. He then guided her to a huge office with glass windows that overlooked the town. His office was filled with expensive corporate furniture and hundreds of books on the law. Daniel motioned for her to take a seat in one of the executive leather armchairs opposite his desk and then sat down beside her. "What can I do for you, Carla?" he asked, with kind and smiling eyes.

"I'm sorry to just come barging in uninvited, but I didn't have your number," Carla apologized. Daniel held up a hand to tell her there was no need to apologize and she continued. "I was single when we met." she stammered out, somehow. "Then we had our... night, and I haven't been with anyone since then."

Daniel looked confused and smiled uncertainly. "I'm not sure what you're trying to say, Carla, he confessed.

"I'm pregnant and it's yours." Carla blurted it out suddenly.

Carla saw a flicker of panic flash in Daniel's eyes. He stared at her in shock and didn't even blink for a long moment, and then he leaned forward and rubbed his hand over his forehead.

"You're sure?" he asked, looking at her with a last ditch glance of hope.

She nodded. "Positive," she said quietly. She knew that both of their lives were about to change forever.

He sat there quietly for a few minutes, his mind spinning with the news that he was going to be a father. Then he looked at her and cleared his throat, laying a comforting hand on her knee.

"I don't want you to panic over this, Carla," he told her gently. "Whatever you decide to do, you have my support. I will give you anything you need financially or otherwise. I'm sorry that this was unplanned. I know you wanted to focus on your business."

"I'm sorry." Carla replied in turn. "It was meant to be a night of no-strings fun and now this..." she sighed and shrugged. "I just wanted you to know."

"I'm glad you told me." Daniel assured her. "Let me give you my number." He began to write down his cell on the back of a business card and looked her earnestly in the eye. "You can call me night or day," he promised her. "There is no need for you to worry about anything. I'll be here and I fully intend to see this through with you. You aren't going to do it alone; that I promise you."

Carla accepted the card from him and felt relief rush over her. She knew that providing for a child was probably not a big financial issue for him; who knew if this had happened before? All the same, she was glad that he was there.

"I don't expect you to drop everything over this," she told him softly, "but I am ready to let you be as involved as you like." She took another business card from his stand and scrawled down her own number. "You should have my cell, too."

Daniel cast his gaze over the digits and nodded slowly. He looked up at her again. "I want you to stay in touch," he told her firmly. "Sonograms, Lamaze classes, doctor's appointments, you name it. I want to do all of that with you."

"Thanks." Carla said, with a tired smile. The last couple of days had been overwhelming, but knowing that Daniel was going to step up for his part of the responsibility was at least some relief.

She had expected an argument from him, or blame, or a discussion about options, but he had offered her simple and unconditional support. She admired him for that. "I better go." she then said. "I left my apprentice alone at the bakery."

"Sure." Daniel said, standing to walk her back to the elevator. "Just know that I am here for anything you need."

After she was gone and Daniel was back in his office, he was able to let the facade slip a little and felt a tidal wave of panic wash over him. This was the first time that a night of fun had resulted in a pregnancy and Daniel had no idea what he was doing. He could offer every financial support to Carla, but they barely knew each other. He didn't want to leave her on her own to raise his child when he had been the one to seduce her that night, but he was also unprepared to be a family man.

His career was on fire, he was dating Brooke, and he liked his expensive apartment with clean walls and expensive gadgets. He just had no idea where a baby or former lover would fit into that picture.

He needed some moral support of his own. He texted Cliff and they arranged to meet at their usual bar at once. His friend was triumphant when he told him the news.

"Ha!" he laughed. "Finally life's catching up with you; welcome to my world, Daniel. What are you going to do?"

"Well, I'm going to support her, obviously." Daniel said with a shrug. "What else can I do?"

"What if you took it a step further? Would you try for a relationship with her?" Cliff suggested. "I've always said that you needed a nice girl for a change. Carla is a nice girl."

"She might be a nice girl, but she's also a stranger." Daniel reminded him. "She's a baker, for crying out loud! What am I supposed to do? Drop everything and buy a three-bedroom place in the suburbs?"

"Don't be so dramatic, Dan," Cliff said. "You're going to be fine. I'm just saying that you shouldn't be so quick to dismiss the idea of a more settled life."

"Hmph!" Daniel scoffed. "I'll support the girl, but I'm not going to be some boring old man with a beard, arguing over the arrangement of the lawn's flowerbed."

"You'd rather be an overworked hotshot hanging onto the purse strings of some selfish brat in a pencil skirt?" Cliff said disdainfully. "I think this is a good chance for you to take a look at what you want for life."

"You used to be a lot like me, Cliff," Daniel reminded him. "Back when you were in corporate law and living the high life, too."

"I sure was." Cliff agreed. "So, I'm the perfect person to tell you that it wears you out. It shortens your life and there is no real quality in a life like that. I'll tell you something, Daniel, I don't ever think back on a single day of that part of my life with longing.

It was fun then, but wouldn't trade five minutes of my life now for a week of that time. You need to think about this. You used to be relaxed. We used to call you 'daring Dan'. You were always having a laugh and acting as the clown. Now you just take life so seriously. You've created this aloof, larger-than-life rich lawyer persona and just don't know how to have fun anymore."

"I thought you were always complaining that I had too much fun," Dan replied. "Now you want me to have more fun?" He frowned at his friend.

"Sleeping with tons of women is not the type of fun I'm talking about, Dan." Cliff told him. "I'm talking about cracking a smile when a joke is funny, instead of barely moving your lips. If an unplanned pregnancy gets you away from the office and back into the real world, then I'm all for it."

Daniel shook his head disbelievingly. He knew that he had changed since college, but he had more responsibilities now. As his reputation had grown, he had not been able to joke around and skip a late night, because that's not how one rises through the ranks of a competitive law firm. Of course, once he started regularly choosing working late over goofing around with friends and chasing corporate women, instead of mixing with all types of people, it did make him change.

Daniel had become much more serious than he used to be; almost untouchable. He decided not to take offense at Cliff's blunt manner, but instead, he chose to give some thought to his friend's earnest words. Perhaps he should offer more than his money and really get involved in the pregnancy and raising the child. Maybe a son or daughter would soften him and give him a reason to smile.

The next day, he told his secretary that he was going to be coming into his office late. He decided to stop by *Carla's Cakes*. It made him smile when he saw the cutout cupcake sign swinging from its frame, with Carla's name painted on it in swirly letters and inside there was a line of people. Behind the counter was a young redheaded girl and then, emerging from the kitchen, Daniel caught sight of Carla.

She was in her element here and that bright smile which made her stand out from the tight-lipped and stern women from the legal world was glowing on her face. She was laughing as she took time to speak with her customers as they ordered and nobody seemed to mind the wait.

In fact, it seemed that some of the customers were just as interested in catching up with Carla as they were in buying her baked goods. She was so friendly and open and Daniel enjoyed watching her brighten up peoples' days.

He joined the line and felt out of place in his expensive suit among all the happy and carefree people gathered there, all talking with one another and seeming at home. Finally, he reached the head of the line and couldn't help but laugh, when Carla looked up, spotted him and exclaimed "Gosh!" with wide eyes.

"What are you doing here?" she asked him with a gasp.

"I wanted to talk to you," he said with a soft smile.

"Oh." Carla looked around her busy store and asked him if he wouldn't mind waiting. He nodded amiably and walked off to stand at the side of the store to wait for her. He was enjoying the time away from the firm; watching people in good moods enjoy good treats.

Finally, Carla was free and she invited Daniel into the kitchen to speak in private.

"I hope you don't mind me dropping by," he said looking around her kitchen with interest.

"No. Is everything alright?"

"I felt like maybe I was too... standoffish with you when you came by yesterday. The news was a shock to me, of course, but I just wanted you to know that I do want to be involved, not just by helping out with costs, but with helping you with the pregnancy and then, when the baby comes, being involved as the father."

Carla smiled widely and she stepped forward to hug him from gratitude. Daniel was surprised by her display of affection and patted her back awkwardly until she drew back. He felt himself blush in the first time since he couldn't remember when. Daniel was great at seducing women, but he still felt like an awkward teenager when a girl wasn't being sensual, but was instead, affectionate.

"That's all I wanted to say." Daniel said, pushing his hands down into the pockets of his pants.

"I'm glad you came." Carla told him with a smile.

The two looked uncertainly at one another for a moment until Daniel said he had to go and waving goodbye to her, he left the bakery. Seeing Carla in her own world made her seem all the more beautiful.

Daniel had thought she was very attractive, but it was when he saw her interacting with other people that he could see that she was also kind and open. She encompassed all of the things that were missing in the harsh business world he lived in. He was still unsure about the prospect of a new baby, but he resolved to do what he could to be there for both Carla and the child.

Chapter 5

It was a relief for Daniel to get away from Brooke's constant complaining and demands for a while, in order to accompany Carla to her first sonogram. He hadn't told his girlfriend about the pregnancy because he knew that she would blow up over it and Daniel was in too much of a panic over the situation already, to deal with her having a fit of rage.

Instead, he just continued with her as though nothing had happened and was grateful for once to have a distant girlfriend as it meant that she didn't notice his agitation or question his absences.

Daniel met Carla at the doctor's office and she smiled shyly at him. She wasn't yet showing, but Daniel was sure that she appeared to be glowing more than before. He greeted her with a kiss on the cheek and guided her into the clinic with an arm around her shoulder.

"Are you nervous?" Carla asked him anxiously. "I'm nervous."

It was twelve weeks since the wedding and for Carla, the pregnancy still hadn't quite sunk in. She felt like she was living in some strange dream, even more so when Daniel put his arm around her. The lawyer was always so calm and collected as though nothing fazed him. Carla wished for some break in his professional manner and something more emotional to show. He reached out for her hand and gave it a comforting squeeze.

"There's nothing to worry about," he told her with a warm smile. "This is only a sonogram."

"To check if everything's OK." Carla added with wide eyes. "What will we do if there's a medical issue?

He stopped short for a moment at her comment and then shook his head. "Let's just hope for one healthy baby." Daniel said with a calming smile.

They entered the examining room and Carla laid on the table and lifted her top to show her slender stomach. The consultant covered her belly in a fine layer of cold gel, prepared the machine, and then began to run the wand over Carla's middle. Carla gasped at the coolness of the gel and reached for Daniel's hand from nerves.

Daniel took hold of it and felt once again that rare shyness that came over him when a woman was sharing genuine emotion with him. He turned his attention to the consultant instead, to shake the uncomfortable feeling of timidity.

"How is everything?" he asked.

"Just a moment..." the consultant murmured. She captured a few screenshots of the image and then smiled reassuringly. "Everything is fine," she told them. "You have one healthy baby in there. It will be a while before we can tell you the gender, but I can confirm the date of conception and give you a due date of the fifteenth of May."

"The fifteenth of May!" Carla gasped. "Daniel, did you hear that?"

"I heard," he said in a whisper.

Carla was disappointed that there was not more awe or emotion in Daniel's voice, but she didn't know that beneath his calm veneer, a strange feeling of longing was beginning to stir. He'd never thought that he'd want children until much, much later, but seeing the screen shots of his tiny bean-sized baby and hearing its heartbeat as it pulsed through the machine, he felt an instant bond to his unborn child and to its mother.

The consultant printed the photographs and handed them to the couple.

"Do you want to keep one?" Carla asked him, offering him a print.

Daniel did, but he knew that Brooke was the nosy type and he didn't want her to find out about the pregnancy through a photo found in his sock drawer or wallet. He shook his head.

Carla didn't understand his indifference. Daniel had said that he wanted to be involved, but he was as hard as steel as he went through the process while Carla was a mess. She felt every kind of emotion coursing through her; fear, excitement, panic, love.

They went their separate ways after the scan and Carla didn't see him again until the following week when he came to pick up copies of her medical bills, which he had insisted he pay in full. She invited him in to wait as she went for the paperwork and offered him a coffee, which he accepted.

She gathered the documents and she laid them on the coffee table of her tiny little sitting room, before bringing out two cupcakes to eat with their coffee and curling up beside Daniel on the sofa.

She was wearing her old jeans and an oversized knitted sweater. If she had known Daniel was coming, she would have worn something more flattering. He didn't seem to notice. In fact, he seemed a little downcast.

"Are you alright?" she asked him.

"Hmm?" Daniel replied. He looked up at her as though breaking out of a trance and looked at her with a vague smile. "Oh, yes, I'm fine." he said. "I've just had a long day."

"Do you want to tell me about it?" Carla invited.

"You don't want to hear about it." Daniel assured her. "It's dull work."

"I thought you said it was thrilling." She smiled at him wryly.

"It can be." Daniel nodded. "It can also be frustrating and endless."

"Tell me." Carla repeated, looking earnestly at him.

The lawyer couldn't imagine that Carla genuinely wanted to hear about his warrants and disclosures and arguments with judges, but she was leaning forward with an open expression and waiting to listen, so he gave in and began to talk.

As he told her about his day and she listened with no judgment, competitive interjections or criticisms, he began to feel some of his pressure drift away and before he realized it, an hour had passed.

"I've been keeping you," he said apologetically.

"It's not a problem." Carla assured him. "I was just staying in tonight. To be honest, it's nice to have some company. It's also nice to get to know you. I mean, it's been a strange start, but you're going to be the father of my child. We are going to be working together for rest of our lives with this baby."

Daniel let out a long breath at the thought. "I've hardly had time to let it sink in." he told her.

"Tell me about it!" Carla said with a light laugh. She picked up her cupcake and peeled off the paper, taking a bite of the sponge and getting pink frosting on her nose.

Daniel spotted it and laughed out loud. Carla was taken aback at the sound. She'd never heard him laugh and her eyes widened in surprise which made Daniel laugh again and he reached over to wipe off the frosting with his thumb. He picked up his own cupcake.

"You made this yourself?" he guessed.

"I did." she said, lifting her chin proudly.

He peeled back the paper and took a bite. He couldn't remember the last time he'd eaten something sweet and simple like a cupcake. He was a vol-au-vent and aperitif sort of man, but as soon as he bit into the frosting, he knew he'd been missing out. He chewed with an appreciative sound and swallowed.

"Amazing. You're good at this."

"I am, aren't I?" she replied with a laugh. "It must be good. You're smiling."

"I smile." Daniel said defensively, lowering one brow at her.

"'I smile'." Carla mocked, mimicking his serious expression.

A genuine smile of amusement formed on Daniel's face. It had been a while since someone had made him laugh. He enjoyed being in the company of a woman who felt comfortable enough to tease him.

Brooke barely felt comfortable enough to have a conversation that wasn't about work.

"I guess I've been a bit overworked lately," he confessed with a tired sigh. "It's hard to shake it off at the end of the day."

"Mmm." Carla sympathized. "It seems to me that you just need to learn to relax."

The baker bit into her cake again and this time got frosting around her lips. Daniel noticed it and smiled again.

"You've got frosting on your mouth." he told her.

"Where?" she reached a hand to her mouth to wipe it away, but missed.

Daniel leaned in to wipe it away again and then, before he'd really thought about what he was doing, he kissed her instead; softly, and sweetly. Carla let him kiss her but when he drew back she stayed frozen in surprise, though her heart was about to beat right out of her chest.

"I'm not looking for anything serious," she repeated in a slow whisper.

"Me neither." Daniel replied, that hungry and haunted look coming to his face once more. She gasped and felt fire burst in her, consuming her with need for him. She slipped her arms around his neck and just like that, they lost control of themselves once again, giving in to that animal attraction that drew them together like magnets.

His hands moved over her clothes and into her hair as he kissed her hotly, growing breathless as his need for her became urgent. She smelled so good, she felt so soft and strong, and there was something about the knowledge that part of him was already growing inside her, that made him need her desperately.

Daniel's lips ran over her ear and neck and he whispered, "Make love with me....," and then he chuckled, "I promise not get you pregnant this time."

She laughed a little, but her body was anxious for him and the smile faded as her lips moved over his skin. They pulled each other's clothes off and worked their way to her small bedroom. She laid him down on her bed and though part of her wanted to indulge in him, her raging hormones demanded satisfaction and the feel of him inside of her. She straddled him and he moaned loudly as she slid his thick erection deep into her, and began to move with him and against him. He grasped her hips and rocked her gently at first, but then harder, and more swiftly as their passion ignited in a blaze. He pulled her toward him and closed his mouth around her dark nipples, sucking and tugging on them with his lips and teeth, making her arch her back and minutes later, she came on him, sighing sweetly and moaning as the ecstasy overtook her.

Watching her like that only increased his hunger for her, and he drove himself deeper into her, pulling her to him and kissing her hard, his hands tight on her body. He lost himself in their heat and pleasure, just as uninhibited and sensually as she did, reveling in the feeling that there was so much more to their connection than just sex. She climaxed again, he couldn't stop himself and he came with her, the two of them reaching a pinnacle together, and then drifting back down to earth in each other's arms.

Daniel and Carla pulled themselves apart slowly and breathlessly, and after some long quiet moments, Daniel got dressed once again. He didn't know if it was the easy conversation with a friendly woman, the indulgence of eating a sweet cupcake or the mind-blowing sex, but Daniel felt more relaxed then he had in years.

He looked at her with consternation and shook his head. "I'm sorry... I just... I don't know what it is about you. I was just going to wipe the frosting from your lips, but then... I needed to kiss you, and..." he smiled at her almost apologetically. Things did not need to become more complicated between them.

Carla shook her head. "Don't worry about it. It just happened. I for one, don't regret it. That was incredible." she leaned toward him and kissed his mouth softly, and then looked at him with her sweet warm brown eyes.

"We'll chalk it all up to pregnancy hormones, right?" she laughed, and a smile spread over his face as well. Both of them were silently agreeing to let it go.

Daniel watched her as she dressed again and he shook his head. She was something else, he thought to himself. He knew he had to go, though, and he stood up, hugging her goodbye.

He was almost reluctant to leave, but he knew that he had a date with Brooke that night and work was waiting for him after that, and so he forced himself to say goodbye.

He should have felt more guilty than he did when he arrived to meet Brooke at the theater after coming from Carla's bed, but as soon as the sulky blonde began to complain about the location of the seats and the temperature of the air in the room. Any shred of guilt he had vanished and as he watched the performance unfold on stage, his mind was still in Carla's apartment thinking of a much more exciting show.

Over the following weeks, Daniel saw more and more of Carla. He started inventing reasons to see her just because his time with Carla in her bakery or at her apartment was about the only time that he felt his life fell down for the moment. He was very skilled at presenting a confident and controlled facade to the world, but it was only with Carla that he truly felt calm.

At four months pregnant, Carla was still incredibly slim and barely showing at all. Daniel's attraction to her was growing stronger every time he laid eyes on her bright smile and beautiful eyes. He loved spending time in her company, with her understanding ways and kind words. One night after weeks of restraint, the two-time only event happened again.

Daniel had been visiting Carla to talk about making plans to buy things for the baby when she felt a cramp in her back and he massaged it for her. His hands moved over her bare skin in a rhythmic motion and with each stroke, heat enveloped them both, and in minutes, they were locked in each other's arms, twisting and turning with one another in her bed, clinging to one another until they both came, lost in their passion and growing emotion.

Lily was the only person that Carla could talk to about her encounters with Daniel. Lily was utterly captivated by the developing bond between them, and practically screamed in frustration every time Carla said that nothing between her and Daniel had changed.

"You should stop hooking up and start, you know, *being* together." Lily urged her. "You clearly can't keep your hands off each other. Why not make it a permanent arrangement?"

"I don't know." Carla sighed. "I don't think he wants that."

"Do you want that?" the girl asked, in exasperation.

"I don't know." Cara sighed honestly with distant eyes.

"How can you not know?" Lily demanded impatiently. "You spend so much time with him now. I can always tell when he visits because you're in a better mood whenever you've been with him. He has stepped up to pay for everything and he's helping out. What's the issue?"

"He has a girlfriend." Carla told her.

"*What?*" Lily exclaimed. "Since when?"

"He told me about her last week." Carla sighed. "He said he's been struggling to tell us about each other. He finally came clean."

"Oh, how noble, after sleeping with you, like, a bazillion times. Oh God! And I was defending him!" Lily said, making a disgusted face. "That's super sleazy."

"It's not like that. He started dating her after the wedding."

"So the other times he slept with you, he's been cheating on this girl?"

"I didn't know about her. You know I wouldn't do that."

"I know that, but obviously he's a cheater."

"I don't think he's serious about her," Carla said with a shrug. "I told him I wouldn't date him, so it's not like he's cheating on me, and they aren't really serious."

"Does it matter if they're serious?" Lily asked with a frown.

"No, I guess it doesn't. You're right. He's a player. I don't want to put my trust in someone like that."

"I'm sorry, Carla," Lily said sincerely. "I thought he was going to be good for you, but maybe you were right."

"Maybe so." Carla sighed.

In truth, Carla had listened to Daniel tell her more than once, since his admittance of her, about how unhappy Brooke made him and she had no idea why he was with the girl.

Perhaps it was because his colleagues, perhaps it was because Brooke was beautiful, or perhaps it was because having a girlfriend made it easier for Daniel to keep his distance from her.

Carla wondered sometimes if Daniel was using Brooke as an excuse not to get closer to her, but she wasn't about to have that conversation with him any time soon. Things were good as they were.

Daniel was being supportive and she enjoyed his company and now that she knew about Brooke, any more passionate encounters were off, so she didn't have to wonder about whether anything more would develop between them. Things were as simple as they could be under the circumstances.

Chapter6

Daniel and Carla spent a day together, shopping for things for the baby. Carla was in her sixth month of pregnancy and although she had a clear baby bump swelling beneath her clothes, Daniel was still enormously attracted to her.

His feelings had only intensified during the time that they spent together over the last four months. He found Carla to be the kind ear for his troubles that he'd been searching for and Carla grew to care deeply for him as he made good on his promise to take care of her.

That day, they were strolling around together through the town when they decided to pop into an expensive department store to take a look at the baby clothing. He was holding an infant's pajamas up to her belly, laughing and smiling with her, and he couldn't resist her beautiful glow. He leaned in to kiss her mouth softly and just as he did, a shrill shrieking caused them to both jump and turn around.

Brooke was standing there with her hands on her hips and her eyes glowering with rage. She cast a furious glare at Daniel, but then she fixed Carla with the most evil stare. Her eyes traveled over Carla's features, over her closeness to Daniel and then settled on her swollen stomach and the female lawyer sucked in an angry breath through gritted teeth and then all hell broke loose.

"Who is *she*?" she seethed, dramatically throwing out an arm and pointing an immaculately manicured finger at Carla. Carla was sure that this outraged woman must be the girlfriend.

Daniel held out his hands to placate Brooke and his voice was calm and patient in reply. He was like the man with a loudspeaker who tries to handle a hostage situation. He chose his words carefully and kept his voice low as he tried to handle the hysterical woman.

"Brooke, calm down," he said gently. "Let's go outside and I'll explain everything."

"You selfish, scheming bastard!" Brooke hissed. "Have you been sleeping with this slut behind my back all this time? How many women do you have? I should have known that a rich guy who kept it in his pants was too much to ask for. Every one of you thinks he's God's gift to women!"

The whole store stopped to turn and stare at the screaming woman and while Daniel kept his cool and didn't flinch in the face of the woman's wild hysteria, Carla grew more embarrassed and angry.

"Stop this, Brooke." Daniel ordered sharply. "You're making a scene."

"*I'm* making a scene? You think *I'm* making a scene?" she shouted incredulously, raising her voice even louder. "Well I have every right to raise my voice when you've been keeping a woman on the side! What, am I not attractive enough for you? Is my

Cornell degree not impressive enough? Or, is it just the fact that you knocked up some cheap floozy that has you walking around the town with her? Could you possibly be any more brazen?"

"I could explain myself if you would step outside," Daniel told her in a firm voice. He gestured to the door, but Brooke was firmly planted and glaring daggers at Carla.

"And who do you think you are, you desperate skank?" Brooke spat viciously. "Got yourself a lawyer, have you? Did you get yourself knocked up to tie down a good thing? Do you think he'd take a second look at you if you weren't pregnant?"

Carla felt the tears of shame and hurt stinging in her eyes and she bristled angrily, barely stifling the tirade of anger that was building in her, but Daniel held her back by firmly taking her hand. Then he stepped up to Brooke and spoke to her one last time in a voice, which was strong, commanding, and unfaltering.

"I find a spoiled ivy-league brat much less appealing. You are embarrassing yourself and me. Don't you dare suggest that she is exploiting me before taking a look at yourself: diamonds, dinners, expensive vacations. Talk about being brazen. Why don't you get off your high horse and leave this store before you make a bigger fool of yourself?"

Brooke's eyes became wide with insult and her face contorted into a furious scowl, and she decided to take her leave, but not before fixing Carla with one last deathly stare, as though trying to remember every detail of her face for when they next met.

After she had left, Carla found that she was shaking from the confrontation and Daniel put a hand on her shoulder reassuringly.

"I'm sorry you had to see that. She is a dramatic woman."

"I guess you never told her about me, huh?" Carla breathed.

Daniel let out a guilty sigh. "I was trying to avoid a scene just like that. I suppose it's better that it's done. No more secrets now."

"Aren't you going to miss her?" Carla asked him with concern.

The lawyer shook his head and laughed a little. "God, no."

The two stood for a moment in the middle of the store, overcoming their shock and then Daniel took Carla by the hand and led her to the department store café for a calming cup of tea and a chance to talk. He bought them both a drink and then sat down with her at a table in the corner of the store. Carla was still angry from the embarrassment.

"She called me a slut," she said with a deep frown.

"She had no right," Daniel told her firmly. "It's my fault. I didn't tell you about Brooke until far too late when things had gone much further with us. I put you in a compromising position and I can't apologize enough. It will never happen again."

"You let her go so easily," Carla said softly. "Did you not care about her at all?"

"You make it sound like I used her." Daniel said.

"Didn't you?" Carla pressed honestly.

The lawyer sighed heavily, shrugged, and lifted his hands in a gesture of acceptance.

"Yes." he confessed. "I guess I did."

"What did she give you?"

"Routine," Daniel told her. "You know, when you hit thirty and you're still single and everyone you know is married and everybody is asking you when you're going to be next, it's comforting to have someone to hide behind. Of course, when choosing a woman to take that role, it always made more sense to choose someone like myself. Unfortunately, I don't get along very well with people like me."

"You felt on display when people were judging you for being on your own." She smiled sympathetically at him. "I get that."

Daniel found himself smiling. "You do, don't you?" It was meant as a compliment. Of all the people in his life who had careers just like his, and social lives just like his, and clothes just like his, it was only to Carla that he felt a true connection and a sense of security.

They were both vulnerable in the same way and it was only through meeting Carla and recognizing her fears of loneliness and of losing all she had built, that he began to recognize that same vulnerability in himself.

They finished their day quickly after that, and Daniel took her home in a taxi, but didn't go up. Carla said goodbye to him in the cab, went up to her apartment, and fell down on her bed with a long sigh. She detested knowing that there was someone out there who hated her. Carla had never had enemies and she did not realize until the next day just how fierce an enemy she had made in Brooke Dawn.

Carla was at work the next day, serving as usual, when one of her regulars, Mrs. Shields, laid down a white flyer on her counter. Mrs. Shields was a plump and motherly woman with chubby cheeks and a wild grey perm.

She always looked windswept, as if she had just wandered in from a storm and she always wore a heavy coat, even in the summer months. Today her face was filled with friendly concern for the nice young woman who had always been so kind to her.

"Carla, honey, have you seen this?"

Carla picked up the flyer and read a message that made her feel sick to her stomach. The piece of paper stated that Carla's bakery did not meet basic hygiene standards and had a whole list of hateful bullet points with false accusations under the accusing headline. Carla had an idea that she knew just who was behind it.

"Where did you get this?" she asked emotionally.

"They're being handed out all over the area." Mrs. Shields told her. "I don't know who is printing them."

"I do." Carla retorted. "Mrs. Shields, I hope you know that none of this is true."

"Of course I do, honey," Mrs. Shields assured her. "This place is always spotless."

As soon as Mrs. Shields left, Carla retreated into the kitchen to wipe away a few tears. Nobody had ever made a target of her before, and Carla was hurt. She'd worked as hard as she could to make her business a success, and to face this attack was a hard blow. Lily followed her into the kitchen with concern and took the flyer from her hand to find out what had made her boss cry. When she read the hateful words, she grew enraged.

"Was this that blonde bimbo who blew up at you at the store?" she demanded. "Who the hell does she think she is?"

Carla wiped her eyes, took the flyer from Lily, and crumpled it in her palm. She sniffed, took a few deep breaths and composed herself, tossing the flyer into the trash.

"She's a woman who's been hurt." Carla replied. "This will pass."

The very next thing Carla did was to call the Department of Health inspector to her kitchen. She had no qualm whatsoever about allowing her kitchen to be inspected and by the following afternoon she had an up-to-date certificate to pin up in her window, citing her excellent hygiene standards.

"That should put people's minds at ease," Carla said to Lily.

However, the very next day, another of her regulars, a young and slim yoga instructor, came up to the counter. She was very upset and confronted Carla.

"Carla, is it true that you don't really use organic ingredients?" she demanded. "I've heard that you're making untrue claims about your ingredients and you know that I love this place because you're fair trade. Is it true that you just use regular ingredients?"

"No, it's not!" Carla gasped. "I get all my ingredients organically and ethically. I pride myself on it. Where did you hear that I was lying?"

"There's a woman at my gym who's been telling everyone that *Carla's Cakes* is a sham." the customer told her. "I was shocked. I told her that I'd always had great service here, but I don't want to buy from you if you're just another unethical chain keeping animals in cages. I'm a vegetarian and I only eat dairy that is organic. I only eat cocoa that's fair-trade. It's a matter of principle, Carla. I don't want to be lied to."

"I'm not lying!" Carla defended herself tearfully. "Tell me, was this woman blonde and really beautiful?"

The customer nodded uncertainly. "Do you know her?"

"Yes, I do." Carla said. "She has a personal vendetta against me. Please don't stop coming here, Trish. You know I value your business and that I uphold the principles you stand for. I have the paperwork that shows where I buy all my ingredients. I can get it right now."

Suddenly Trish was contrite and the tone of her voice became kinder.

"No, I trust you, Carla, she said apologetically. "I'm sorry to have come in all guns blazing, but a lot of corporations make false claims about these things to attract customers. I always read the fine print and it's simply because I love this place so much that the rumor upset me."

"Well, it is just that." Carla told her with a smile. "A rumor."

In the weeks that followed, Carla had a steady stream of customers coming in to complain or question and when some familiar faces stopped walking through the door, Carla felt her heart break and the next time that Daniel came to see her, she found herself sobbing on his shoulder.

"She's ruining my business!" Carla wept. "She's out to get me!"

Daniel held her in his strong arms and did his best to soothe her. He felt such guilt for having caused conflict for Carla who was innocent in all of it and who had worked so hard to become successful.

"I won't let her get away with it." he promised.

"What are you going to do?" Carla asked him tearfully.

"What I'm best at. I'm going to sue the hell out of her."

"Sue her?" Carla repeated. "For what?"'

"Libel, slander, loss of earnings and emotional trauma." Daniel retorted. "Because that's exactly what she has done."

"I don't want to sue anyone..." Carla faltered. "I just want her to leave me alone."

"Trust me, Carla." Daniel warned, "That woman is like a dog with a bone. She won't let go. Her ego has been bruised and she's out for blood. She works with big clients and she knows what makes a business go down. She's building a mob mentality against you.

There's no smoke without fire and soon people will stay away just because they've heard one too many stories about this place."

Carla began to cry heavily at the thought of her business falling to pieces and turned into Daniel's shoulder to weep. He stroked her hair tenderly and comforted her with promises.

"I'm not going to let it get to that point," he vowed. "I am filing a motion today. I will run her into the ground. I will make her pay for this."

"But this is our fault!" Carla retorted. "We cheated. She's acting out because she's hurt."

"She's acting out because she's not used to not getting her way." Daniel retorted. "She's poison. Don't feel any pain for her, Carla, because she's not hurt, she's insulted and none of this is your fault. *I* cheated. You didn't know about her because I kept it from you. I am the only person to blame in all of this, but I will not let her hurt you or your business. You have my word."

Carla had been made promises by other men before, but when Daniel made promises to her, she believed him. She nodded and sighed.

"What do you need me to do?" she asked him.

"I need access to all of your records." he told her. "I can prove that every one of these claims is a false accusation. When that's done, I will have a hard case that everything that has been said is libel and slander. Then, all I need to do is trace the rumors back to her and she's done. She is not a well-liked woman. I'm sure there are plenty of people dying to throw her under the bus."

"I don't want you out for blood, Daniel." Carla told him earnestly. "I'm not looking for a fight."

"I know you're not." Daniel said gently. "You're not a vengeful creature. I, however, do not take attacks on me or mine lightly. She's started a war because she knows that I'll bite. Let her just wait and see. I'll demolish her. She's loaded enough that she'll be able to take the hit. I'll deal with this, Carla."

Carla did not want to cause trouble, but Daniel had a look in his eye that she had come to recognize as the gleam he got when he had the heart of a case in his hands. She knew that it would not leave again until he'd tasted victory.

There was nothing she could do now, but let him fight in her corner and hope that he fixed things before too much damage was done. Her business and her happiness were in his hands.

The abuse and rumor-mongering escalated in the weeks that followed. But Daniel was meticulous in his work and as she prepared the things he needed as evidence for his case, she got to see him at work. She was in awe of his ability to track down witnesses, get ahead of the opposition, and that incredible encyclopedic knowledge of the law he had, which allowed him to always come out on top. Not long after that, they had a date set for court, just weeks before Carla's due date.

Daniel saw Brooke just once in the time before the case when he passed her on the main street on his lunch one day and she stopped pointedly to confront him once more with a satisfied smirk on her face. Daniel had no time for her games and his face formed a scowl at the sight of her. He stopped too and they squared off against each other like two boxers in the ring.

"You are out of line, Brooke." Daniel told her harshly. "What do you think you're doing, hunting down an innocent woman because you're insulted? I didn't hurt you; you couldn't care less about me. It's childish and this has gone way too far."

"Innocent?" Brooke hissed. "She's been opening her legs to another woman's man and you're defending her like she's a saint."

"She didn't know about us." Daniel told her. "She is innocent."

"No matter. You'll be the one to have to deal with the guilt when I rip her and her pathetic little pie-stand to shreds."

"You don't stand a chance, Brooke." Daniel told her. "You'd better quit while you're still in once piece. You have my office number. If you decide you want to settle, I'm all ears. Otherwise, I'll see you in court and I will *tear you apart*."

"You've got nothing on me," she snapped at him nastily.

Daniel did, in fact, have a quite a bit on her. He managed to get the electronic records for the photocopier, which traced her user ID as the one which had printed the flyer. A certain young associate who'd had no sympathy from her after her brother's death, was more than willing to testify that she had seen Brooke making the copies, and that she, herself refused to hand them out when ordered to by Brooke. Of course, Daniel didn't tell Brooke this, he just simply smiled to himself and walked on.

He hated that he had caused this unnecessary stress to Carla, especially when she was getting to the later stages of her pregnancy, but he was glad to have the right set of skills to be able to help her now.

Brooke had picked a fight with the wrong man. Daniel was a lion in the courtroom. His record for victory in court surpassed all others who had graduated alongside him. He was considered elite even among the elite; the best of the best. He had been the youngest lawyer at his firm to bring in his own corporate client and his tenacity and drive had served him well ever since.

He made the big bucks because he was a winner and his success hadn't gone unnoticed. His name was on the lips of everybody who mattered in the legal profession and soon an opportunity would come his way that made him question where his own loyalties lay.

Chapter 7

Since the confrontation with Brooke in the
department store, Carla had done her shopping alone.
On this day, she was browsing for strollers in a local
mother-and-baby store when a handsome man several
years older than her, who'd noticed the look of
confusion on her face, approached her. He was a tall
man, with kind green eyes and salt-and-pepper hair.
He was wearing a pair of denim jeans and a knitted
sweater. He looked like the sort of model you'd seen
in a *Good Housekeeping* magazine.

"You look confused." he said, approaching her with a
friendly smile. "Can I help?"

"Do you work here?" Carla asked uncertainly,
looking for a nametag and finding none. Her question
made the man laugh and he shook his head.

"No, but I've already done this twice." he told her.
"I'm actually looking to sell one of my old strollers,
but it has a busted wheel so I thought I'd come by on
the off-chance they could tell me where to get a
replacement. The *E-Z-Stroll 360°* is not a reliable
model, let me tell you."

Carla smiled at his advice. "How old are your kids?"

"Eight and six." he told her. He pulled out his wallet
and opened it up to show her a picture of two
adorable little girls. "They're great girls. Both very

creative. Sophie is the brains and Laura is the chatterbox, and you? Have you been married long?"

The baker laughed out loud at his presumption and shook her head with a knowing smile. "No." she said, patting her stomach meaningfully. "This one was a little unexpected."

"So you're single then?" the man asked her.

"I suppose so." Carla said with a light laugh. "And you? Married?"

"Divorced." he replied. He held up a hand to show her the pale ring around his ring finger where a wedding band had used to be. "Things were great at the start, but life changes you. We started arguing and just thought it was better for the girls if we parted ways. That was two years ago now."

"It must have been a tough decision."

"It's never Plan A to divorce," the man agreed, "but sometimes it's the lesser evil. Like you. I guess it was a hard decision to be a single mom."

"It's not quite like that." Carla said. "The dad's involved."

"Is it romantic?" he asked with purposeful curiosity.

"A very, very brief romance." Carla said with a wry smile. "Now he's just there to support me, but we're not an item. He had a girlfriend until very recently."

"So if I asked you on a date that would be appropriate?" the man sad tentatively. "Although I suppose I should introduce myself first. Geez, I guess you can tell it's been a while since I did this. I'm Michael."

"Carla." Carla replied, smiling at his shyness in asking her out. He was a fatherly, slightly awkward man, but Carla found there was something comforting in being around someone who'd already been through those tough years ahead that she was facing.

"Well, Carla, I'd love to take you out sometime for a non-alcoholic drink." he said playfully. "We could talk more about the wonders of parenthood. I have some excellent tips."

"Are you bothered by the fact that I'm expecting?" Carla asked with a surprised laugh. "Most men would run for the hills at the sight of this bump."

"Things don't always go according to plan." Michael emphasized. "Still, I don't get the opportunity to meet many women and I've always been a family man myself. I love kids. I've been through a divorce. I'm not afraid of a few complications."

Carla thought about it for a moment. On the one hand, there was Daniel, but since finding out about Brooke, Carla had kept clear of him in terms of any sexual involvement and he had not made any advances towards her.

Things had settled between them and as much as she still felt the chemistry and had come to admire him as a lawyer and as a man, and even more so as a friend, she couldn't hedge her bets on the off-chance that he'd give up playing the field and settle down with her. He just didn't seem the type and Carla had to admit to herself that being a single mother would not help her find a man.

Daniel had once told her that circumstances sometimes find you dating someone just like yourself, because it makes life easier than trying to find someone who might bring surprises and that's where Carla felt she was.

Daniel was no safe bet, but a nice single father who understood her troubles and spent his afternoons in stroller shops might be just what she needed right now to get her life back on track. Despite the fears that remained, Carla nodded. In her position, she couldn't afford to turn down any offers.

"Wonderful!" Michael said enthusiastically. "Could I please have your number?"

Carla programmed her digits into his cell and smiled at the big, goofy grin it brought to Michael's face. It was clear that he did not have that confident streak that Daniel had, but maybe Carla needed someone a little less infallible.

Meanwhile, new paths were opening in Daniel's own life. Carla's due date was nearing and so was the court case, but now something else was brought to the table to make Daniel question everything.

Stephen Turner was a brilliant young lawyer with whom Daniel had studied at Harvard. They'd graduated the same year, but their paths had rarely crossed. Daniel had been the first in his year with Stephen just snapping at his heels.

Matthew Pike was an older gentleman with many years' experience in the law and very deep pockets. Daniel was surprised to get a call from Stephen one day, inviting him for drinks and even more surprised when he found the well-known Matthew Pike at his side.

Daniel recognized him as a guest speaker he had heard in his second year of college and when he entered the restaurant, he was quick to shake his hand in respect. Pike had been the one to win the infamous *Preston vs. Dyke* case and helped an underdog company overthrow a multi-million dollar corporation. He was legendary. Daniel shook Stephen's hand too, and the two lawyers invited him to take a seat at the table.

Stephen was a fair-haired young man who wore large, square glasses like Clark Kent and who had a habit of nervously drumming his fingers against any nearby surface. Matthew was a man in his mid-fifties with tightly curled black hair and a brooding expression. He had the same defiant spark in his eyes as Daniel and he set those eyes upon Daniel as Daniel took a seat opposite him and Stephen.

"Good afternoon, gentlemen," Daniel said. "I must say, I'm curious as to why I'm here."

"You shouldn't be." Pike replied matter-of-factly. "You must have expected headhunters to come tracking you down eventually."

"Headhunters?" Daniel repeated uncertainly.

"We're starting a new firm," Stephen told him pointedly, drumming his fingers against the pristine white tablecloth. "Pike's current partner passed away last year and he's decided it's the right time to make a break from *Dunelm & Pike* and start afresh."

"*Dunelm & Pike* is behind the times." Matthew told him. His voice was sharp and he spoke his words in short and pointed sentences which emerged like bullets from his mouth, clearly a habit born from years of stating facts in court rooms and using his tone for emphasis. He spoke as though he were the narrator for some very serious and intellectual film as he spoke about his own aspirations. "Ryder is gone, Dunelm is nearly dead and everybody else is incompetent, greedy or both," he said bluntly. "*Dunelm & Pike* is dying. There is too much conflict within the firm. It's losing focus and the business just isn't coming in, out here away from the city.

We need to be in the midst of it all where the real corporate giants are. I want to start again in the city with new premises, a new attitude, and fresh blood on the team. I need sharp minds and lawyers with energy and drive. Your reputation precedes you, Mr. Towler, and after considering many other talented lawyers, Mr. Turner and I have decided that we'd like you to be our third partner. *Pike, Turner & Towler*. What do you think?"

Daniel was left speechless. The opportunity was gigantic and something that he had been working towards his entire life. Matthew Pike was a legend. Stephen was one of the best there was among his generation of lawyers, and both were asking him to get on board with a partnership that could catapult them to success.

With Pike's experience and pull, Stephen's eye for finance and Daniel's skill at bringing in new clients, they would make an unstoppable team and Daniel had always known that his future was in the city.

Except, now, his future was also in a tiny unborn child that he'd promised to raise. He gave it a moment for the shock of the proposal to sink in, cleared his throat and began to ask questions.

"What's the timeline on this proposal?" he asked, looking at Pike.

"We begin founding the partnership today," Stephen replied. "We move premises in three months. We bring in clients from month four. We win our first dynamite case month six. Bam. We're in business."

"Wow. This sounds like an incredible opportunity." Daniel stammered out.

"You seem unsure, Mr. Towler." Pike commented. "Is there something holding you back?"

"I have a child on the way," he confessed. "The partnership is my dream, but the timing is a little... off."

"When's the child due?" Stephen asked him.

"Two months."

Stephen and Matthew exchanged glances and Matthew sat back in thought. His jaw moved up and down as he considered the options as though he were literally chewing on ideas and at last, he spoke.

"We want you," he said at last. "This is how it is: We're going to be in the city in three months. We want you there. I say that you take your time to think about it until your kid is born. In the meantime, we'll track down premises and begin to set up the firm. By the end of June, we'll be ready to open doors. Stephen and I are going to talk to our second choice lawyer and tell him you are on the fence.

On the first of July, we open doors for business. If you're there, your name goes up on the wall. If not, it will be someone else. Does that sound fair?"

"More than fair." Daniel said eagerly. "Thank you, sir."

The trio discussed a few more details and then left after another round of handshakes. Daniel was left shaken by the encounter. Going to the city as a partner of his own firm was beyond his wildest dreams. Most lawyers couldn't hope to achieve that kind of seniority until well into their fifties.

Of course, it would be a new firm, starting from the ground up, but that was the kind of challenge that got Daniel's heart pumping and made him feel alive. He would get to work alongside the best and brightest and work with some of the most prestigious clients in the market. It was all he'd ever wanted.

Then there was Carla. Daniel had grown more than fond of her during the pregnancy. She had a calming effect on him and made him laugh when nobody else could. He couldn't imagine life without her now, but, then again, his career had always been the very essence of who he was.

He decided that the only thing to do was to sit Carla down and have a frank discussion about their options. Perhaps things would work out if he only spoke to her and broke from his usual habit of keeping everything from the women in his life. He hailed a cab and headed to her apartment.

When she opened the door to him, she looked pleased and greeted him with a platonic kiss on the cheek, inviting him in.

"How are you, Daniel?" she asked him brightly, sitting him on the sofa and getting him a cup of coffee and a cupcake.

"I have some news," he told her.

"Me too!" she beamed.

Daniel smiled. Even though he was bursting to tell her what was on his mind, he also loved to hear about her day, especially when she was smiling like that, and so he invited her to speak first.

"I met someone today." Carla confessed. "I know because of our history that maybe that's a little strange to hear, but if this whole mess with Brooke has taught me anything, it's that it's best to be honest about these things."

"You've met someone?" Daniel repeated. He felt his stomach drop and his words turned to lead in his mouth. He no longer wanted to speak about the potential to go to the city or anything else on his mind. He wanted to know who had the gall to hit on the pregnant woman who meant far more to him than he'd ever admit. "A man?" he added needlessly.

Carla laughed at the way he said it and nodded. "He was at the stroller store."

"You went to the stroller store without me?" he lowered his brow.

"You said you had a business meeting."

"I did."

"Well, anyway, I was at the stroller store and this nice guy; a divorced father of two, just started talking to me and we kind of hit it off. He's going to take me for a coffee to give me some advice about the pregnancy and having a newborn."

"He can't be that nice if he's divorced." Daniel muttered.

Carla's eyebrows shot up in surprise at the tone of his voice. "Are you jealous, Daniel?" she asked him.

"No!" he snapped a little. "You can do what you like."

She turned to face him more fully with an upset expression on her face. Daniel instantly felt guilty to have put it there. Carla had said not a word against him even when she had found out that he'd slept with her while dating Brooke and he had no right to be jealous of her now.

"We've spoken about us a hundred times,' Carla said carefully. "You told me it wasn't what you wanted."

"It's not," Daniel replied quickly. "You're great, Carla, but we're just too different. We'd be fools to force something just because there's a baby on the way. We have to stay logical, even when we're getting emotional."

Carla rolled her eyes. "You never get emotional."

Her words hurt. Even now, Daniel felt like everything was falling apart. He was on the precipice of a great victory, but also on the precipice of a great fall. He could leave and chase his dreams, but break his promise that he would be there for Carla and leave his child behind, or he could stay, miss out on the one opportunity life would give him to fulfill his potential, and watch the love of his life grow close to another man. He swallowed back his feelings because he was not a man to show such things and he stood up to leave.

"Daniel!" Carla exclaimed. "Where are you going? You haven't even touched your coffee."

"Work." Daniel mumbled angrily.

"You said you had news for me," Carla reminded him. "You came all the way here, so it must have been important."

"News?" Daniel repeated. His mind went blank for a moment as he searched for an excuse to be here and then found one. "I've got another witness for the case."

"That's great." Carla smiled. "Thank you."

Daniel simply grunted instead of telling her that she was welcome and let himself out with barely a goodbye. He strode away from the building in a foul mood. Inside her apartment, Carla had no idea what she had done to make him so irritable.

Was Daniel really so upset that she'd been asked on a date? He'd had months to make his move and hadn't done anything. She'd watched him date that blonde bimbo and was now suffering the consequences of his relationship, and yet she had never said a word, so how could he be so callous now? Carla called Lily to talk about it.

"So he came in, heard about the date and stormed out?" Lily summed up after hearing the tale. "Wow, that is one love-struck pup."

"Love struck?" Carla scoffed. "It was more like he was angry with me. I guess it's because he doesn't like complications in his life. He told me that's why he was dating the bimbo. He just likes things to be predictable and routine and I suppose that me having my own life is just too much for him to handle."

"Don't take it that way, Carla." Lily replied. "He's definitely into you, like, crazily. I mean, you've told me that he never smiles and never shows emotion, like he's a statue, cool as a cucumber, but as soon as you meet someone else he flips his lid? A man who can keep his head in court and in a department store when a vile woman is screaming at him, but loses it when a woman he spends a lot of time with wants to spend time with someone else is very clearly in love. It's jealousy, Carla. Pure and simple."

"Do you think?" Carla asked her uncertainly. "I mean, Dan's just so hard to read. He never lets anything show. I think it's the lawyer in him. He's trained to have this poker face, but sometimes I just want to see what's really going on underneath. I get glimpses of it from time to time when he forgets himself and starts laughing or when he gets excited about the baby and breaks character for a moment, but most of the time he just pretends that nothing can touch him. It drives me mad. I just want to know where he's at."

"And where are you at, Carla?" Lily asked meaningfully. "Is he a fling, or just the father of your child or something more?"

"All of the above." Carla sighed. "I admire that man. I care about him. He's been nothing but kind and supportive through all of this. He's not the player I thought he was; there's been nobody since Brooke, and he's doing everything with the case to save the bakery out of his own good will. There's so much good in him.

Yes, I think I love him a little, but that's no good if Dan doesn't feel the same and there's just no way to tell. I'm in a position where I'm about to have a kid. I'm getting older. I can't be turning away men just in case Daniel lets me in someday. Michael is a kind, sweet, and open guy. I know what he's thinking. I know he likes me. It's plain, it's simple, it's easy. What's wrong with wanting simple and easy?"

Lily sighed on the other side of the line. She didn't really have an answer for her. "I guess if you think this new guy will make you happy..." she pondered. "I just don't want you to make a mistake. You're crazy about the lawyer. I know you are. I know you like everything perfect all the time, but sometimes a little madness makes life interesting, you know?"

The Final Chapter

It was the day of the court case and Carla was waiting anxiously at home while Daniel battled on her behalf in court. She kept looking down at her cell phone in the hope that Dan would call, and twisting her hands together nervously. All of the gossip and nasty rumors about her bakery had taken its toll on her emotionally and on the business. She just wanted it all to be over.

Suddenly, there was a knock on the door and Carla looked up at the clock to see that it was already the mid-afternoon. She raced to the door and pulled it open to find Daniel standing there with a rare grin on his face.

"We won?" Carla gasped.

"We won!" he told her happily.

"Daniel, you're amazing!" Carla gushed, rushing to him and throwing her arms around his neck. "Thank you!"

The lawyer accepted her hug and held her closely to savor the embrace. He'd become more comfortable with Carla than with any other woman he'd ever had in his life. He let her go and walked over to her tattered old sofa. He sat down and began to tell her what their victory meant.

"She was found guilty of all the charges." Daniel explained. "The judge has granted a restriction order against her and any further harassment will be liable to criminal charges; which means prison. She was also ordered to pay compensation for lost earnings and trauma. It's a lot of money, Carla."

He pulled out the figures from inside his suit pocket and handed them to her. Her face fell in shock and she looked at him with wide, disbelieving eyes.

"Are you serious?" she asked him breathlessly. "This kind of money for some spurned woman's bitchy actions?"

"She knew exactly what she was doing, Carla. It was a vindictive vendetta and the judge saw right through her. You had a good lawyer. I told you I'd run her into the ground."

"This has to bankrupt her." Carla said with sudden panic in her voice. "The restriction order was enough. We shouldn't take this."

Daniel couldn't believe her selflessness and concern even after all she'd been through and he felt an almost overwhelming surge of affection for her which was turned bitter by his knowledge that she was seeing another man and that he still had to make that terrible choice. Suddenly the smile fell from his face, but he tried to keep his mind on the problem at hand and reassure Carla.

"This is a drop in the ocean for Brooke." He promised her. "Take the money and use it to build up what she couldn't tear down."

"I don't know what to say, Daniel." Carla confessed emotionally, wiping a tear from her eye. "Thank you." She smiled at him and hugged him tight.

The next day at work Carla told Lily all about the win and the redheaded apprentice was just as incredulous at the sum.

"You told me he was good, but that's just ridiculous!" she gasped. "He must be a wizard. A court room magician."

"He's something." Carla agreed.

"What are you going to do with all that money?" Lily asked her.

Carla sighed guiltily and prepared to confess something to Lily that she made her swear not to mention to anyone. Lily could sense the weight of the gossip and leaned forward across the counter with eager eyes.

"Tell me!" she squealed impatiently.

"You know how I always keep checking out premises in the city, you know, just in case?" Carla asked her.

"Of course." Lily nodded. "You've been fantasizing about opening a second store there forever."

"Well, there was this one place right in the middle of the city. It's the perfect location. Even with this win the cost is out of my price range." Carla said. "Still, I put in a ridiculously low-ball offer on the off-chance that I could get it.

I know that a store like that in the perfect place just won't come up again. There's not another coffee shop or café on the whole street, but it's right on top of a whole bunch of offices and there's a bookshop and a music store..." She sighed longingly. "It's just perfect."

"It sounds amazing." Lily agreed. "But what about Daniel? What would you do if the offer was accepted?"

"It won't be accepted." Carla said assuredly. "I just made an offer on the off-chance. It won't be considered."

"But if it was?" Lily pressed. "And not just Daniel, what about Michael?"

"Gosh, I hadn't even thought about him." Carla realized with a guilty gasp.

Lily rolled her eyes. "Of course you haven't." she agreed. "Because you're madly in love with Daniel. I dunno why you're with that old man."

"He's thirty-nine."

"He looks a hundred." Lily teased.

"He's handsome," Carla said generously.

"He's no Daniel."

Carla sighed and thought about the consequences of leaving both men. She didn't think that it would matter much to Daniel. In the weeks that she'd been dating Michael, he'd become so distant and moody with her that she felt like she wanted to get away from him.

Michael, on the other hand, was very sweet, but he just didn't get her heart thumping or her blood running the way that Daniel did. He was a safe bet, but dull. Now that Carla had tasted passion and electricity, anything less just left her feeling unfulfilled and she longed for another night with Daniel, but Daniel wasn't interested.

"There's no sense in discussing it." Carla said at last. "It's not going to happen."

Although Carla was thinking a lot about the premises in the city, she soon found that there were going to be much greater things on her mind when her contractions started on the seventeenth of May, only two days after her due date.

She had been in the bakery when her water broke and it had been Mrs. Shields and Lily who helped her waddle into the kitchen away from the customers and call Daniel in a panic. Then they called an ambulance and she was whisked away to the hospital where Daniel was anxiously waiting for her.

It was the first time that Carla had ever seen him look nervous. He paced the corridors anxiously, rubbing the back of his neck and drinking obscene amounts of coffee from the vending machine to keep himself from thinking about the baby that was on the way.

When a maternity nurse finally informed Daniel that it was time, he entered into the delivery room at Carla's side and squeezed her hand as she pushed their daughter Maria into the world.

After the parents and friends and relatives came to gather around and coo and offer their congratulations, Daniel and Carla were finally left alone. Carla was enchanted by her daughter, but equally enchanted by the look of wonder on Daniel's face.

His mask had slipped and she saw underneath it a man captivated by the sight of his newborn baby girl. He held her, and as he looked down at the tiny little face of his beautiful daughter, with her dark skin, dark hair, and his grey eyes, Carla swore that she saw him tear up for a moment, which made her heart well with joy because it showed he was not made of stone.

"She's beautiful." Daniel said in a voice that was husky from emotion, although he quickly cleared his throat to rid his voice of the tenderness there. "Are you alright?" he asked her, looking at her in concern.

"I'm fine." Carla promised. She reached out to lay her hand atop Daniel's and looked up at him with an exhausted but triumphant smile. "She's our little girl."

For a few days after the birth, Daniel could not have been more attentive, more supportive, or more loving of Carla and her daughter, but after she was out of the hospital and back in her apartment, she noticed the lawyer beginning to return to his sulking ways. In fact, she noticed him change his attitude the very second he heard that Michael would be visiting.

"Michael!" Daniel seethed. "It's not the best time."

"Michael and I are a couple now, Daniel." Carla replied gently. "Is that going to be a problem?"

In her voice was a silent plea for him to break character, break down, and tell her that he loved her. Instead, he grew stubborn and turned his back on her.

"Do what you want."

That was the way it was. Carla didn't know if Daniel was acting out because he was hurting, longing, or selfish, but there was simply no way to tell with him. Meanwhile, her relationship with Michael was ambling along, but Carla could tell that it would soon be on its last legs.

Although there was nothing outwardly wrong with the relationship, it just felt like there was no chemistry in it either. It meant that when she received a call from a property agent when her daughter was just three weeks old, Carla decided to leave.

She didn't tell Daniel right away that she was leaving for the city, for the same reason that he had never told

Brooke about the pregnancy. She didn't want a big angry scene that was just too much for her to handle. Carla felt like she was in a place where Daniel didn't want her, Michael wasn't right for her, and she needed to take her chance for happiness where she could find it.

She would get around to telling Daniel when the time was right, but for the time being, she confirmed her offer and began to get the paperwork for the move underway.

Meanwhile, it was the middle of June and Daniel was running out of time to make his decision. He was desperate to go to the city and fulfill every dream he'd ever had. Every time that he thought about making the call to Pike and Turner to tell them that he would accept their offer, his thoughts would turn to his little girl Maria, and to Carla; to her gentle eyes, bright smile and kind and caring ways.

He would think about how, despite all the drama and surprises, that he had never felt more himself, more calm or less alone than since he'd met her. He realized that no matter how much he loved the buzz of the courtroom and the thrill of building a fearsome reputation, it was sharing it with Carla that made it all feel worthwhile.

Without her, the manic corporate world was hectic and he often reaped great rewards, but they began to feel empty since Carla started to date Michael and wins felt less like wins when Daniel couldn't tell Carla about them and have her share in his victories.

He missed having a companion who didn't just want him for his money or reputation, but for all the things he was. Never once had Carla been jealous or dependent or spiteful. She was beautiful and humble and loving. She was his better half and he needed her.

He made his decision. That day he left his office at half-past two and headed across town to her bakery. He walked in past the customers, past the wide-eyed Lily, and into the kitchen where Carla was whisking up a batter. She looked up when she saw him standing there with such determination in his stance and longing in his eyes, and then suddenly he was telling her all of the things she'd ever wanted to hear from him.

"Carla, you are everything that is good in this world," he announced loudly. "You are kind and gentle and humble and you see the good in people all the time. I've accepted women who have wanted me for all the wrong reasons and I have chased women that I have wanted for wrong reasons all my own.

I have told myself for years that committing to a woman would ruin everything that I had built for myself and that it would mean I had to make a choice between everything I've ever wanted for myself and being with her."

He took a few steps toward her. "Well, that time has come now. I have been offered a partnership in the city; a chance to be a named partner at my own firm. It is the fulfillment of my life's ambitions two decades early and everything I ever wanted.

I have only two weeks left to tell them I'm on board and yet, every time that I go to make that call, all I can think about is Maria and you, and the way you make me feel and suddenly everything I thought I wanted doesn't matter, because everything I truly want is right here. I want you, Carla. I love you."

The whisk fell from Carla's hand and her eyes filled with tears. She began to laugh from happiness and relief and as she stared at Daniel, she saw everything that she loved in him. He was strong, capable, and he made her feel safe. He never backed down or shied away from a problem and his calmness and control made her feel like everything would be okay, no matter what was happening. When they spoke, she felt like he truly heard her and she felt special every time that she drew a smile from him when nobody else could.

All their lives, they had both been looking for someone who fit in with what they thought they wanted, without realizing that loving the right person makes all those desires for career success, fortune, and glory, seem trivial in comparison. Carla wanted him desperately wanted him too.

"I thought you didn't want me," she confessed emotionally. Daniel crossed the distance between them and stood before her, breathless and determined. He shook his head meaningfully.

"I want you more than anything. I want you more than a partnership. I want you more than the city. I love you, Carla. I choose you and Maria above all those other things."

Tears of joy were now running down Carla's face and she threw herself into Daniel's arms. Those arms which had once been so slow to return her affections now tightened around her and she felt all his coldness become warmth and all the distance between them vanish.

"You don't have to choose."

"What do you mean?" Daniel asked with confusion.

Then Carla explained to him about the store in the city, about how she was ending things with Michael and about how she had been ready to run away at the thought that he didn't want her, but was now overjoyed that he had finally told her how he felt.

"We thought we were such different people," she said through her happy tears, "but we're both heading in the same direction. Let's go to the city, Daniel. You, me, and Maria. Let's build our lives without having to choose. We can have it all."

A radiant grin broke out on Daniel's face and he swept her up in his arms to kiss her with a kiss that wouldn't lead into the bedroom, but would lead into a full and happy life together. Finally, he'd met that one person who could transcend everything else.

Carla had come into his life and disrupted it, but, somehow, he'd still ended up exactly where he needed to be, but with a future laid out before him that was more satisfying than anything he could have ever imagined. Carla was breathless from her joy. She had it all. She would get to open a new store in the city and start a family with a man who loved her, and who she deeply loved.

One year later, Carla and Daniel were at a wedding once more. Daniel helped her carry in the wedding cake with the poker table bridge-and-groom cake topper into the main reception where Lily rushed into Carla's arms to greet how old friend.

"Congratulations, Lily!" Carla beamed.

"It's so good to see you!" Lily gushed. "I was afraid you wouldn't make it, what with the bakery doing so well in the city."

"I wouldn't have missed it for the world," Carla said.

That evening when Daniel and Carla danced, it was with everything exactly as it should be and then, after the party was over, Daniel asked Carla to walk with him in the beautiful grounds of the exquisite manor that Lily had hired for the day. Daniel walked her down a tree-lined path that was strung with glittering fairy lights that twinkled in the darkness.

"It was a nice wedding," he thought aloud, "but one thing kept bothering me."

"What's that?"

"Well, I couldn't help but think that it should have been you and me up there getting married." he said. He bent to one knee and produced a beautiful diamond ring, which sparkled under the fairy lights. Carla gasped and her hands flew to her mouth. Her Daniel, who was so bad at the romantic gestures, loved her enough to ask her to spend her life with him.

"Carla Bennet," he began with a big grin that came so much more readily to his face these days, "will you marry me?"

After all the ups and downs and chaos in their relationship, there was now no doubt left in Carla's mind. This man made her deliriously happy.

"Yes!" she exclaimed.

Daniel slid the ring onto her finger, raised himself from the ground and embraced her, pulling back only to kiss her passionately.

From there, life only got better. Carla conquered another town with her bright smile and cupcakes, and Daniel built up a fierce reputation in the big city. Maria grew up happy and loved and in time had a little brother joined her. Neither Carla nor Daniel would have pictured their lives turning out so perfectly, but their love affair taught them that sometimes giving into something completely different, is entirely worth the risk.

THE END

Authors Personal Message:

Hey beautiful!

I really hope you enjoyed my novel and I would really love if you could give me a rating on the store!

Thanks in advance and check the next page for details of my other releases. :)